NAKED GRAVES

Natalie Townsend

NATALIE TOWNSEND

JESSICA HUTCHINSON

Table of Contents

Acknowledgements

❝ *The fact that you're even reading this right now is amazing. I appreciate you taking the time to dive into this adventure of a story with me. I'm so proud of myself for turning my ideas into something tangible, but I never could have done it without the support of my friends and family. I dedicate this novel to the ones who truly believed in me throughout my entire life, especially through my writing. You know who you are. I'd like to give a special shout out to my fur baby, Ronald. Without you, life would have little meaning. I love you, Moo-Moo.* **❞**
Natalie

NATALIE
TOWNSEND

❝ *Thank you for picking up this rollercoaster of a book. I hope you have as much fun reading it as I did writing it. However, this was not easy for us. Two different minds, two different opinions, and two different time zones. Believe me, it was a rollercoaster for us, too. Being the introvert that I am, writing has always been a good outlet for me, though poetry is my usual genre. I certainly never thought that it would ever amount to anything, especially not the thing you're holding in your hands, but here we are. I am so excited and I can't wait to hear your feedback. I would like to dedicate this book to my sister. Through everything in my life she has always been my biggest supporter, always checking up on me to make sure that I'm okay, and always ensuring I know she is there for me no matter what. She is the reason I had the confidence to follow through with this book. Alongside her, I of course thank my mom, my dad and brother: all of you are the best family I could ever ask for. You all let me know how much you love me everyday, and I love you all so much for that.* **❞**

Jess

JESSICA HUTCHINSON

DANDELION

Hope, Love, and Happiness

Wednesday, June 8th, 1966

A ***devastating tornado hit Topeka***. I remember I was lying on my bed when I heard the sirens start to blare. My Mama barged in, screaming at me to get up and move as quickly as possible. We had a small underground shelter about 30 feet from the house, with food and water stocked. As we were running to it, I looked up at the sky and saw an indescribable color I've never been able to match to this day... The best I can describe it to you is a dusky olive and faded black color. I could see objects being thrown around in the distance. It was captivating—almost impossible to look away from— which is why I'm thankful I had such a wonderful Mama to protect me from the flying debris.

That monster of a storm was unlike anything I had ever

seen and I was terrified. I knew Mama was scared but whenever I glanced at her, somehow she had the calmest look on her face throughout the entirety of the storm. That specific tornado was rated an F5, which is as intense as it gets. There were hundreds, maybe thousands of people injured from it... luckily we weren't among them.

Though I wish that my father, Asshole (I like to refer to him as that, seeing as that's the first word that comes to mind when thinking about him), would have been among the injured, sucked up and spit out far away from us. The storm destroyed over 3,000 homes. Basically the whole town if you ask me. How did we not get hit, you ask? Who the hell knows. My Mama told me it happened in just 26 minutes, but how can that be? I just didn't understand at the age of 19.

Friday, September 17th, 1967

The very last time I would walk out the doors of that broken-down ranch, and the last time I'd see my good-for-nothing father, too, or so I thought. Who gives a shit about him though?

It was the last time I would ever see my wonderful mother. It was her that I cared about—Lynnette Marie Soyles. I never even got to say goodbye.

I woke up on the floor with a bleeding gash on the back of my head. I knew he must have taken a swing at me. Let me tell you, a fireplace shovel to the head is the worst headache you'll ever have. I'm not even sure why we had that damn thing cause we didn't even have a fireplace. It's not something that you can forget, ya know?

I looked over and saw my mother lying on the kitchen floor, hair a mess, her face black and blue, blood pouring out her nose and mouth, her neck turned just a little too much to the left. I knew as soon as my eyes came back into focus that he had killed her. He broke her neck and killed my Mama. What an awful way to leave this world, and for what? What did she ever do?

A bouquet of flowers lay scattered and torn around her, some petals stained with flecks of her blood...*Those fucking daisies.* Paul used to bring my Mama those flowers as his way of apologizing every time he fucked up. Each time he tossed her those handpicked sorries, it made me despise him more. Did he really think they would make anything better? Seriously... Does anyone truly think that some plants could ever change things? I mean, I came into contact with flowers practically every day at one point in my life. Flowers meant for the dead, meant to express love, meant for people who haven't the slightest clue that they're even receiving them. What a waste of money, paying for something that you could just grow in your own backyard.

It's not like those who've died get to admire the flowers, or smell them, or even watch them wither, so why squander your time and money?

Why do anything if you know it's completely pointless? Perhaps people hope that the colorful life and energy of the plants will bring back their loved ones. I don't *hope,* though. I never have and I never will. I *know* that she is never coming back, and there is nothing I can do about it.

Perhaps it's not the flowers or my pitiful excuse of a father that I despised. Maybe it's that I never had anybody to give flowers to. I wouldn't even know *how* to send a bouquet today. Everyone from that wretched September day is long gone now. Except me. I'm the only one left to ponder my bad decisions and figure out what I'm gonna do with the rest of my meaningless life. Somehow I ended up alone in possibly the smallest town in existence; Meerdin, Delaware. That's where I called home for many years, until I... uh, relocated... I'll humor you with the details of my once-unappreciated life.

It was the late '60s, early '70s. Life was good and free; I miss that feeling sometimes. Ya know, freedom. Anyways... Meerdin...about 30 miles outside of Dover, was barely a speck on the map, with a raging population of 641. The population decreased significantly over my stay, but I'm sure it's surpassed 700 now... ever since I left.

Pretty down-to-earth people there, ya know. One of those places where you can't go to the market to buy eggs without running into someone who knows your name. The buildings are all the same—mahogany brick that wraps its way across the 84,000 square feet of the entire town.

Aside from the flat bricks, Meerdin has some beautiful spots to see like the bayside drive on Route 9, Grand Isle Beach, and some mountains. The sunsets are uncanny when you're standing at the peak of a giant rock. However, I never got around to watching them much in my life. Other than that, it's a very flat state. Certainly no tornadoes rolling in and out of nowhere, like Kansas.

All in all, not much to do around that small town; it's what you make of it. *Anything can happen while nothing happens at all.*

There was this one tiny alleyway in between Klaus and

Orrin streets that seemed as if it went on for miles and miles. It was my secret smoking spot most nights where I would go to think. Actually, it was my smoking spot every night. Come to think of it, I had the same routine every day for my first two years there.

6:00 AM: *Wake up and brush my somewhat stained teeth with baking soda.* It was cheaper than paste and Mama always said it would make 'em sparkle. I tried to floss, but who was I kidding? No one has time for that before work.

6:30 AM: *Make my way to the local post station and pick up the papers for the day.*

7:00 AM: *Start my morning route.* Ya, I was a 21-year-old paperboy that made 80 cents an hour. Definitely not the greatest job but it paid the $110 monthly rent and the three packs of Dovals I smoked a week.

Bad habit, I know, but something had to take up those awkward moments when I was forced into an unwanted conversation with that old woman from down the street who always stopped me. Never caught her name... that I can remember.

8:47 AM: *Deliver the morning post to Ms. Ingrid Freya-Robbins,* the most beautiful woman in all of Delaware. I'd never forget her name. She was Mr. Robbins' widow (she just couldn't give up her maiden name since her parents were millionaires), the man who shot himself in the head in 1962. I never knew him but she talked about him sometimes. She also got all his money when he died, which made her even more rich.

9:30 AM: *Continue my paper route* after finishing my third cup of chamomile tea from Ingrid. I miss Ingrid. She was something special, something genuine—no doubt—and to this day I still crave chamomile tea routinely at this time in the morning.

10:00 AM: Around this time, I'd be riding my bike too quickly over the railroad tracks right after the Pike Ave traffic light, and bail out. All my newspapers and shit would dump all over the road cause the tracks were too shaky, and nobody would come to help me. Every fucking morning, the same thing... I never tried to conquer the tracks either. Maybe I just didn't care. Or maybe I liked that life kept giving me the same shitty 10 AM struggle. Maybe I enjoyed being able to do something besides just throwing the papers onto someone's porch. Who knows. Sorry, I'm getting sidetracked. Side-*tracked*? Hah. Get it?

10:15 AM: *Stop at Lloyd's Locals,* where I scraped my change for a 60-cent pack of Dovals and an apple. Surprisingly they pair pretty well.

12:40 PM: *Breathing Game.* I'd pass the local cemetery every day at this time, and I'd always try n' hold my breath from the "Meer Murphy Creek" sign to the last tombstone, which had to have been a quarter mile. Think I only completed this task a total of 17 times in my whole paperboy career. Just goes to show you what smoking eight Dovals a day does to the lungs.

12:41:18 PM: *Take a breath.*

1:00 PM: *Finish my deliveries for the day.* Probably could've finished two hours before if it wasn't for my nicotine addiction and the daily tea distraction of that beautiful cougar.

1:35 PM: *Scott's Bar.* Time to pay my daily visit to the local bar on my way home, right next to the building that had been vacant forever. There I swallowed a swig of Scotch with my buddy, Scotty, the owner of the bar. Scotty. Scotch. Scotty. Scotch. Scotch. Scotty. Hah... haha Scotch. Scoo-otttt. Scotch. Never had more than one though, cause Asshole showed me what happens when you have more than one.

2:45 PM: *Bike home* (adrenaline pumping) cause the ride made the shot hit me as if I'd had two or three and I always thought about how much of the day I still had left to do absolutely nothing with.

3:30 PM: *Have my daily conversation with my neighbor, Fay,* in the hall upon her return from work. Always the same: "Graham! So good to see you, dear. How was your morning?" Fay always shouted at me, despite the fact of my standing 10 inches away from her. "Same as yesterday, Fay," I muttered, as we swiftly brushed shoulders. She went into her apartment on the right, and I headed up my first flight of stairs.

3:45 PM: *Take a nap.* I'd slip under the covers of my twin-size, stained bed where I'd try to forget how terrible my life was and dream about when I was young.

Whenever I'd remember the dreams, they were always the same. I saw my mother with her signature grin on her face, running through a field of dandelions, laughing and appreciating life. It felt like time stood still.

I noticed every aspect of her face as if it was my first time ever seeing it. That brown, straight hair, those bushy eyebrows that didn't quite match the color of her hair, her beautiful green eyes that stared back at me like I'd done something wrong, the lips that she used to kiss my cheek every night and say to me, "...everything will be okay because tomorrow is a new day. I love you Graham Embry Soyle, and I always will..." Then I'd see a flash of deep red. I saw the cold laminate flooring, and I saw all of my mother's beautiful facial features smeared with death...

5:30 PM: *Wake up* from my nightmare, and walk outside to smoke a much-needed cigarette and check back into reality. The evening breeze made it easy to do so.

Typically, I felt joy from watching two chipmunks—they lived in the tree in front of my balcony—chase each other back and forth.

6:00 PM: *Start to decide what I want for dinner.* Usually, I had four options: 1) Save food for the next day and skip dinner for the night; 2) Knock on Fay's door to see what she was cooking for supper. She always made enough for two, even though her husband passed three years prior, and she'd usually share; 3) Heat up some white rice and pinto beans that I kept in the cupboard. The white rice had no flavor (kinda like the shit I eat now) but if you scooped two piles of rice, and one spoonful of beans, a flavor was created that would slide down the throat with ease. Cheap and easy; 4) I'd splurge and cook the chicken breast I bought once a week with a potato.

7:00 PM: *Eat or don't eat.*

8:00 PM: *Cigarette break.* Time for the after dinner smoke. I saw once in a documentary that the reason a person craves a cigarette after they eat is because the act of eating and the act of smoking are the same, in that oxygen is lost in the process. So, since people don't typically eat nicotine-filled sticks for dinner, they're not taking any in when the oxygen is lost from the consumption of food.

Therefore, the human body craves the nicotine fix that

it was surviving without for the full course of the meal. Anyway... True or not, I went with it! I always smoked two Dovals because I never started feeling that slight buzz of nicotine 'til the last draw due to (maybe) having some food in my stomach. I can remember starting the second one, eyes closed, deep breaths. I held it in for a good eight seconds. That's when I'd really start to feel it.

8:30 PM: *Take a walk*. After putting on my torn, scratchy burlap bodywarmer—a washed-out navy blue—I'd depart for my evening walk.

Seeing as this was the most adventurous part of my day, I was always excited to venture off into the nighttime air. Sometimes I'd even bring a can of Little Kings to sip on. One was enough for someone who's not much of a drinker, and lucky for me they were pretty cheap.

Typically, I took a right at the "Clover Apartments" sign and headed down McCormick Lane. I walked on the side of the road in the grass with no shoes on because I liked the feel of the grass blades in between my freakishly long toes. Five or six automobiles usually passed on the road, always the same ones so I got the chance to get to know the drivers; Todi especially. He was the only Korean man in Meerdin, and always stuck his caramel-skinned hand out the window of his rusted Ford and waved at me as he sped past.

I took sips of my beer, trying to make it last the entire walk, in increments of street signs. Every four signs I passed, I took a huge gulp and savored every trickling drop of liquid that ran down my throat. I walked the one-and-a-half-mile distance to Scott's bar, contemplating on going inside and drowning my life away with whiskey, just like my father did. I'd put my clammy hand on the door handle, and just stand there a few seconds.

In my head, I heard my mother's soft voice once again say "...everything will be okay because tomorrow is a new day..." and I'd turn around and head home. Besides, I'd see Scott the next day for my after-work shot anyway. I'd finish my last gulp of Little Kings next to this unfinished bench while enjoying my last cancer stick of the night. I'd place the can of beer on the sidewalk and stomp on it, and toss it like a frisbee into the lake. Pretty sure they called it the "lucky Lake of Wishes." Rumor has it that one wish will be granted to whoever takes a dip at the break of dawn. I have yet to test the theory. One day, perhaps.

9:30 PM: *Bedtime*. I would strip down to my tighty whities, and climb into bed, hoping to not have the same dream from earlier that day.

So yeh, that's what I did every day from the time I moved from Topeka to Meerdin up until the time I was given a new interest.

WEDNESDAY, MAY 3RD, 1969

I was making my paper deliveries somewhere between 10:30 AM and 11:00 AM, when I heard the faintest sound up ahead. It was a—

It's time for lunch! I must go. Will return soon, hopefully.

Graham Embry Soyle
09/08/06

LILIES

Purity and Fertility

Friday, September 8th, 2006

This is the current day and for some reason I am thinking about grade school and how I wish I was still in it. Something I never thought I'd say... See, I don't remember much about school because I wasn't really interested in it. I was focused on Delilah for so long during those years... s'pose she made it better. The only actual material I remember learning in school would have to be social studies, specifically just the state capitals. Don't ask me why, but I had a special talent when it came to memorization or anything that required organization skills. I mean, flawlessly I could sing the answers in less than five seconds every time. I even came up with little rhymes or certain sayings to remember them by. Ya know it's clearly something you'll never forget cause I still remember all my little cheats and tricks. See, the capital of Minnesota is St. Paul... so just remember that *Saint Paul bought a mini-soda* (mih-nih-sOH-tuh). Oh! And...ummm... the capital of West Virginia is Charleston so just remember that *Charles lives in the West and he is a virgin that weighs a ton!* If you get really creative, that one would also help you remember the capital of Virginia! Just think of the same virgin from the West, but now he moved away from the West and he became rich... so that gives you Richmond, Virginia! Fuck! I could do this all day. It's just as fun as it was when I was learning it. I remember that was the only test in my whole school life I ever got a 100% on. And then capitals were gone and I had nothing to be good at anymore. Yeh I still enjoyed social studies the most, but I missed my favorite topic. Let me share with you my easy system for remembering the U.S. state capitals:

Alabama (Montgomery)—*Imagine there is a mountain in Alabama named "Mount Gum" and it is airy at the top...* so put it all together and you get "Mount Gum Airy" or "Montgomery."

Alaska (Juneau)—*It's June in Alaska all year long!* Not really, but ya get the point. June...Juno...Juneau. Do the math.

Arizona (Phoenix)—*The phoenix flew straight to Arizona when he hatched.*

Arkansas (Little Rock)—*Arkansas has little rocks.*

California (Sacramento)—*When I went to California last week, I bought a sack of mementos to remember it by.* "Sack of mementos" = "Sacramento."

Colorado (Denver)—*Just pretend for a moment that*

you have a cousin named Vern but everybody calls him Ver and he lives in a den in the mountains of Colorado. Ver in a den...Denver.

Connecticut (Hartford)—*I bought my first Ford in Connecticut and it sure stole my heart... or hart... Hart... Ford...*spelling mistakes are necessary when memorizing the U.S. capitals.

Delaware (Dover)—Well, I will always remember this one now because I lived in the state for so long but when I was a kid I used to remember it by saying, *"I dove into my new life in Delaware."* Looks like that actually came true for me...

Florida (Tallahassee)—*I make a tally mark everytime my dog, Hassee, shits on the couch.*

Georgia (Atlanta)—*The true Atlantis is probably in Georgia...* that is utter bullshit, but it helps me remember! I'm pretty sure I put "Atlantis" on my test instead of "Atlanta" a couple of times but Mrs. Ahles never marked it off.

Hawaii (Honolulu)—Ok, this one was always hard for me. I ended up actually learning this the old-fashioned way by just writing it down a bunch of times, so that is what I recommend for anyone struggling like I did. Or you can think of the phrase, *"homosexuals live in Hawaii and they're all lulu (cuckoo)"*... so "Homolulu" = "Honolulu."

Idaho (Boise)—*Boise potatoes are grown in Idaho.*

Illinois (Springfield)—*In the spring, the noisy fields of Illinois make me ill.* Yeh, this one is a jumble of words. But, just do some rearranging and you get to the final outcome. Spring. Nois. Field. Ill. Springfield, Illinois.

Indiana (Indianapolis)—Easy. If you can't remember this one, then you have problems you didn't even know you had.

Iowa (Des Moines)—Des Moines means "monk" in French if you didn't already know... *so I owe a monk some francs.*

Kansas (Topeka)—This was an easy point in school because it was my hometown, but for those of you who need a little help: *Climb to the TOP of a mountain with a can and toss it off with sass while yelling "EKA!."*

Kentucky (Frankfurt)—*Kent ate a Frankfurt in Kentucky.*

Louisiana (Baton Rouge)—Baton Rouge means red stick in French, so... *Just think of Louis and Ana playing with a red stick.*

Maine (Augusta)—*It is August in Maine all year long.*

Maryland (Annapolis)—*Mary owns a land, Anna owns a metropolis.*

Massachusetts (Boston)—*My new boss, Mr. Chusett, weighs a ton. Boss...ton... HA!*

Michigan (Lansing)—*Lance can sing? I don't know.*

Minnesota (St.Paul)—*Saint Paul bought a mini-soda!* Duh!

Mississippi (Jackson)—*Jackson could never spell Mississippi without saying it out loud every time. M-I-S-S-I-S-S-I-P-P-I!*

Missouri (Jefferson City)—*Miss Jefferson moved to the city.*

Montana (Helena)—*Helen and Ana moved to the*

mountains in Montana.

Nebraska (Lincoln)—*Abraham Lincoln was born in Nebraska.* Yeh, this is definitely false. Pretty sure Nebraska wasn't even a state at the time... but whatever... it helps with memorization.

Nevada (Carson City)—*I bought my son a car in the city.* Car–son...City.

New Hampshire (Concord)—*My favorite wine is Concord Grape shipped from New Hampshire.*

New Jersey (Trenton)—*The new trend is to wear a ton of jerseys on top of each other.* Trend-ton, Trend-ton, Trend-ton... say it really fast a few times and the "d" starts to become obsolete.

New Mexico (Santa Fe)—Just pretend like Mexico doesn't celebrate Christmas the same way as America does and so they call their Santa, "Santa Fe." Then just remember that you're not actually talking about Mexico Mexico, you're referring to *New* Mexico of the U.S.A.

New York (Albany)—Ahhh New York... everybody wants to guess New York City for this one... Manhattan... the Big Apple. Just think of all of that, and then forget everything you ever knew, because THAT IS NOT THE CORRECT ANSWER. *It is very simple, actually. Albany. "A" is for "a lot of people," "L" is for "lots of people," "B" is for "bustling people," "A" is for "annoying people," "N" is for "noisy people," and "Y" is for "yelling people." Got it?* Ok, good.

North Carolina (Raleigh)—Yeh, I always get the north and south states mixed up... honestly you just need to learn these. All I've got for you is *Carol liked Leigh because he lived up North.*

North Dakota (Bismarck)—*Dakota liked Marck because he lived up North.*

Ohio (Columbus)—*A bus full of Columbians are on their way to Ohio.*

Oklahoma (Oklahoma City)—I'm not even going to give you a hint.

Oregon (Salem)—Scramble the letters in Salem and you get "males." *There are a lot of males in Oregon.*

Pennsylvania (Harrisburg)—*Harris had a special pencil (Pennsyl) with burgs all over it.*

Rhode Island (Providence)—*There are a lot of dents (dence) in the road (Rhode).*

South Carolina (Columbia)—*Caroline moved from Columbia to the Southern United States.*

South Dakota (Pierre)—*Pierre moved from France to South Dakota.* Like I said, I've got no advice on the north and souths.

Tennessee (Nashville)—Are you from Tennessee, because you're the only ten *I* see. Sorry, I've always wanted a reason to say that. Shit. I don't know. *Pretend like you're ashing your cigarettes in Tennessee and cigarettes make you ill.* So, that gives you "Ashill." Just add the "N," "V," and "E" and you've got Nashville.

Texas (Austin)—*Three of my exes are named Austin.*

Utah (Salt Lake City)—Utah is a 4-letter word. Salt is a 4-letter word. Lake is a 4-letter word. City is a 4-letter word. *Utah has a lot of salty lakes.*

Vermont (Montpeiler)—Easy. *Vermont. Mont*peiler.

Ends with *-mont*. Starts with *mont-*. *Mont Mont Mont Mont...* then just add peiler. Like... *I'm peeling a mont.* Whatever a mont is. If a mont is even a thing.

Virginia (Richmond)—You're gonna meet "Charles the Virgin" a couple lines down from West Virginia. Think of the same man... but he moves out of the West and he loses his virginity and is rich now.

Washington (Olympia)—*If only washing a ton of laundry was an Olympic sport?*

West Virginia (Charleston)—Remember, *Charles lives in the West and he is a virgin that weighs a ton!*

Wisconsin (Madison)—*A con about living in Wisconsin is that Madi, my son, commits sins every day.*

Wyoming (Cheyenne)—*"Shy Ann" (Cheyenne) lives in Wyoming.*

Sorry, I got distracted. Now as I was saying before I was interrupted last, on May 3rd, 1969, I heard a whimper up ahead somewhere. It sounded like an animal was hurt, or in desperate need of help. I increased my speed a bit to get closer to the sound as quickly as possible. I skidded through some leaves as I rounded a sharp corner and almost ran over what looked like a rolled up ball of wrinkled bed sheets. If it hadn't been for my quick feet and functioning bike belts, this story would have a totally different ending. I did stop, though. Actually I must have stopped more quickly than I thought, because it threw me onto the rocky cement road, catching my knee along the way. The gravel went straight through my only pair of faded jeans, creating a large gaping hole right at the seam of my lower right pant leg.

The mysterious object that I was so curious about ended up being a dog and he was just looking at me laying on the ground with his big, beady, crusty eyes. I could tell he hadn't eaten in a week, or been cared for in months, maybe years. His fur was so knotted up, I could barely tell he was even a dog. His nails needed trimming, his eyes needed flushed out, and the poor thing just needed a long bath. I assumed that a dog that had suffered that much trauma would be afraid of a lot of shit, but to my surprise, this small pup was full of joy. He was ecstatic to see me and I couldn't pass up an opportunity like that. "He could be my first friend, my first pal in Delaware. I mean, shit, it has been two years and the only friend I have made so far is Scotty, ya know aside from my daily acquaintances: Fay and Ingrid. It would be nice to have a companion with me to go on morning paper runs, and... he could accompany me on my nighttime walks!! Yes. I need him. I want him as my own. What will I call him? Lassie? No, I can't call him that. I could call him Betsy, the name of the cow I got for my eighth birthday in Kansas! No, Betsy is a girl's name. I know! I will name him Gene. He is the reason for the loss of my blue jeans today. I ruined my jeans, and then I found one Gene. It's perfect. Gene is perfect!" I thought.

Little guy ended up becoming my partner in crime from that day forward. I carefully stuck him in my satchel and finished out my morning paper route for the day, and then took him to his new home. I filled up my bathtub with room temperature water and gently lowered him in, not knowing how he was going to react; but he loved it and started realizing that he had somewhere to call home. I scrubbed him down with some moisturizer that someone gave me as a "tip" on one of my paper deliveries, cause that was all he had at the time. Oh fuck... I remember that feeling when I realized the extra cost that was going to come with having a new friend. I was gonna have to buy dog shampoo, dog food, bones... I thought about getting a second job! For the time being though, he was happy with the extra scraps from whatever I ate for dinner.

After bathing him, I truly saw him for what he was. A quirky porcelain white rat-dog with one oversized dark brown spot on his lower back. He had ears that looked like they were meant for an elephant and they flopped down almost to the floor. I cut his nails the best I could with some old scissors I had in the kitchen drawer, and sanded them down with this cardboard box that had been laying under my bed for months. His eyes reminded me of galaxy-like black marbles and his nose was such a dark shade of pink, it almost looked red, with one tiny dot on it—almost the shape of a heart.

He just needed one last finishing touch and he would be ready to take on the world with me. I took the scissors that I had just trimmed his nails with and cut a two-and-a-half-inch wide slice of fabric off of the bottom right leg of my pants. Then I double knotted it around Gene's neck, making sure it was tight enough to not come off, but loose enough to make him comfortable. I then wrote "GENE" with a Sharpie on his handmade collar. I stopped and stared at his cute ears and toothy grin upon his snout, and thought to myself how lucky I was to have heard that little whimper earlier that day.

Thinking about Gene makes me realize how normal my life was for a brief moment...how normal my life *could* have been if I just let it be. I can't even imagine being so normal. What could I have done to prevent certain events from happening?

I want to be the same as everyone else: normal. I want to be normal but then again, I don't. Or maybe I just don't know how to be. Besides, normal is boring. Graham is exciting. Yes, I just referred to myself in the third person and yes I know that might seem a bit weird or crazy to you "normal" readers, but let me tell you something. Don't read this beautiful biography that I'm writing about myself... that I'm pouring my blood, sweat, and tears into... if you consider yourself NORMAL.

Put yourself in my handmade toilet paper shoes for a moment and be crazy. Be crazy with me. That moment (the one where I tied Gene's jean scarf around his tiny little neck and looked into his galaxy eyes) is the moment I decided it was clearly time for a change in my life. I wanted to spice up my daily routine a little bit and not do the same old shit every day. I wanted to make memories with my best friend, my partner in crime. I wanted something to live for, something that I cared about, something that I was obsessed with—anything really. So I walked through life with an open mind from that point on, willing to try anything that crossed my path, ready for the next step in my life.

SATURDAY, JULY 19TH, 1969

Gene and I were out taking a walk after eating chicken and stuffing for dinner. It was a good day: our bellies were full. Well, as best they could be I guess compared to most days. The moon was shining bright, crickets could be heard dancing in the distance, and the air had a calm sense to it. I felt at peace. Sometimes when I'm having a bad day in here, I think back to this exact summer night and try to envision the same scenario, the same peace and serenity of the air. Usually my attempts at feeling peaceful are overpowered by cold flooring and unnerving noises from down the corridor. However, back to Gene. He loved the outdoors. He liked when we walked different routes because he got the chance to sniff new territory and piss and shit in new unique locations.

We made it a long distance that night: all the way to Meer Murphy Creek. I had never walked this far on my usual nighttime strolls. I had only biked past the cemetery on my paper path, but I knew the no-breathing rule still applied. I informed Gene of the rule.

Whether he understood me or not, I felt like I was experiencing something with a friend. So I took one large breath of the crisp summer air and ran with him past the Murphy Creek graveyard. Of course, Gene went ahead and decided to take a piss break right in the middle of the game; I was quickly running out of breath. I didn't know what to do—if I should continue the game or not.

But I figured I can never make it to the end anyway, so I'll just quit. Just like everything else in life, I guess I don't try hard enough. I glanced over at Gene and saw that he had pissed on what looked to be a picket sign in the grass. I decided to take a peek. "NOW HIRING" in bold red lettering. That's what the wood sign said right underneath the cemetery entrance sign.

"What an interesting job that must be, more so, than throwing papers at people's doorsteps every morning, and it probably pays more than what I make at the post. Perhaps this is just what I need right now," I thought out loud.

The only memory that was flushing my mind at that moment was how I never went to Delilah's funeral. How ashamed I was. Graveyards always made me remember her and all the guilt I had buried inside me. I just couldn't bear to go, ya know? Wait, I'm getting ahead of myself. I'll get back to her later.

So the next day after work, instead of taking my ritual shot with Scotty, I went straight to the cemetery, knocked on the office door, and applied. I had decided earlier that morning that that would be the last day I ever delivered a newspaper anyway, so I didn't even *want* the job anymore. I *needed* it. The woman who was there to interview me was a friendly, short little old lady who smelled like a kindergarten teacher. I wouldn't have known what she smelled like had the aroma of her perfume not been so strong, and I'm still not sure how I knew it was the same smell my teacher had every time she'd walk past me; I just knew.

It sent me straight back in time to when things were much simpler, which in turn allowed me to have a good feeling about that stout little woman and the outcome of the upcoming interview. Her voice was so gentle and nurturing. She had short wavy hair, the color of a snowflake. Wrinkles, but not enough to make you think that she was older than, maybe 55? Her name was Bettie Murphy. She told me the business was left to her around the age of 17 when her parents abruptly passed in a tragic accident. She didn't want to tell me any specifics and that was fine by me. She told me the last person that worked there had been there for around 30 years before he decided to finally retire. She essentially wanted someone to take over the place for her, seeing as she had no kids of her own to pass it to. She apparently lived a long lonely single life and had nobody. Sounded like a pretty good gig to me. I already had so many ideas rolling through my head within seconds of her telling me that. Oh, what I made of the place! I had no idea what the future held for me in that family-owned graveyard.

Bettie showed me the proper way to dig a grave. About three feet wide, eight feet long, and six feet deep. She said it should take about four to five hours to dig a hole with those dimensions; five or six if it were raining and a little longer than that in the winter cause the ground is tougher to break through. She expected the graves to be dug within 24 hours of service request, for the leaves to be raked once in the morning and once before sundown. When I finally asked about the wages, she said that she would start me at $4.50 an hour. $4.50 an hour?! I was going to be a king. The king of Meerdin who is able to afford rent, dog food, Dovals, Scotch, some tasty food items, and still has extra money to spare!

I didn't even care what she said after that, I knew I wanted the job. Maybe that's why I didn't hear her when she said not to touch the graves of the dead. I couldn't really help it, though. The interview consisted of walking around the entire cemetery. So of course I got a little curious and reached down to caress one of the stones that stood out to me.

The reason it caught my eye was because it had a Chinese symbol placed in the middle of it, or Korean? I wondered what it meant. It might have been one of Todi's relatives for all I knew. Maybe that's why he was in Meerdin to begin with. I met Todi a couple of times; one time I was on my break having my Scotch shot and he walked into the bar and sat right next to me. He ordered water. "Kamsahamnida" is about the only Korean word I ever learned, because of him. Apparently it means "thank you." Anyways, Bettie quickly tapped my shoulder, telling me it wasn't polite to touch a stranger's tombstone. So I stood up and we kept walking.

I woke up on Wednesday morning at seven o'clock with a huge grin on my face because Bettie had told me at the end of the interview that the job was mine if I wanted it. I don't think it was too hard to get a job back then; but I was just ready to start my new life. I had a different dream that night while I was sleeping. I saw Paul, the fucking asshole whose semen created me without my permission, sitting on his ass drinking whiskey right out of the bottle. Not a surprise from that scumbag. He was just staring at me while I rubbed his disgusting feet.

I was 11 and didn't know any better. I didn't know how to stand up for myself and say no. Mainly, I was just scared. He would spit on me if I ever stopped rubbing, even if it was just for a second because my little thumbs were so tired. And the second my mother was finished scrubbing the pots and pans, he would tell her to get on her hands and knees and switch with me. He wouldn't spit on her though when she stopped. He would just bash her over the head with whatever he had in his hand or on the table next to him.

I guess it wasn't really a dream, but more of a memory from my stupid fucking childhood, and I remember it like it was just yesterday. Sorry, I try to watch my language like my Mama taught me, but when I'm talking about him it just seems to slip out. Anyways, the reason I woke up so happy that Wednesday morning was because after my mom started rubbing Asshole's feet in the dream, I pulled a shotgun from mid-air and shot Paul Robert Soyle in the goddamn face. Too bad that part didn't happen in real life....

I threw on my ripped-up jeans and a white t-shirt, 'cept it was more of a brownish color now. Ya know that sweaty looking brown color that stains everything? Well, it was the nicest outfit I owned. I placed Gene in my satchel and trotted out the front door. I basically skipped all the way to Lloyd's Locals and bought a pack of Dovals. I reached for an apple but remembered that it was a new day and a new life, so I grabbed the banana next to the register and completed my purchase.

Yeh yeh, some might say, "New day, new life, new cigarette brand," but there's no way I was ready for that yet. Non-smokers just don't realize how difficult it is to switch cigs. Small steps are better than no steps at all.

I walked to The Creek and checked in with Bettie to see what tasks I had for the day. I asked her in the interview if it'd be okay to bring my pup to work cause I didn't wanna leave him home alone all day.

She agreed as long as he behaved himself. It was a hot July morning and I figured I might be getting a little sweaty so I made sure to put on extra deodorant this particular morning. I had completely "forgotten" to buy a jug of water at the market, thinking I would just dehydrate and end all the bullshit early and head for the afterlife. That day wasn't all that bad, so I decided to stick it out for another day. Bettie told me what my chores were and I quickly wrote them down on the back of my receipt from Lloyd's incase I forgot. I saved it too so I would never forget:

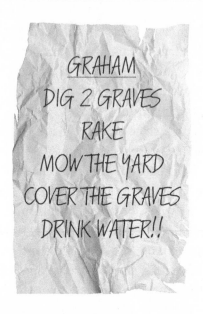

Seemed like I would be able to manage everything there, except for the last one, of course. I'm pretty sure Bettie saw the worry on my face cause she handed me an empty jug and said, "There's a hose in the back behind the tool shed." I walked over to the tool shed and filled my jug with warm water, mainly for Gene. I then proceeded to open the shed and grab a shovel out of it. There were three shovels inside, one that was eight-feet long, and two that were six-feet long. Behind the shed, I saw another small building, larger than the office space, but definitely not bigger than a small convenience store. I asked Bettie, "What is that building for?" I motioned towards it with my hand, "behind the shed over there" and she proceeded to tell me this long story that went along with it. She told me a man by the name of Vern lived inside of it.

Bettie said that her family would see him everyday be-

34

cause he would sleep outside of Murphy Creek on the sidewalk and they got to know him over the years. He was partially blind, and lived homeless his entire life—or so they thought—so The Murphy Family let him live in the building behind the shed as long as he helped every now and then with some tasks around the cemetery. I became somewhat close with Vern over the years, and came to respect him as the special person he was.

There was a complicated process that went into digging the graves in the correct spot and I wasn't sure I was ever going to figure it out. Bettie created a chart with all of the graves on it and where they were located in the yard. Every grave was meant to be six feet apart in distance from each other as to give the spirits some privacy or something like that.

So, the first grave in the yard is six feet away from the bounds of the yard, and the second grave is six feet away from the first. That's easy enough right? I walked over to the last grave that was dug and the last body that had been buried there, "R.I.P. Meredith Grousher, Mother, Wife, Friend, you will be missed, 1912–1969," is what the tombstone read. Upon the bed of dirt that lay six feet above the coffin buried below rested a bouquet of orange lilies. It got me thinking about that time I gave someone a bouquet of lilies.

SATURDAY, MARCH 3RD, 1962

I was fifteen years old. Lanky and awkward, with my jet black hair that I inherited from my father. Or so I thought.

Wish I would've got my Mama's brunette hair, but ya can't get everything you want, I suppose. I had piercing green eyes—well, I still do have those I guess, just not as handsome anymore. However the jet black hair has changed significantly over the many years of not being able to get a haircut or buy a pack of dye at the market. Man, I hate seeing it get gray. Kind of like how I met Vern for the first time.

Anyways, I went to Polka High in Topeka, Kansas, named after Richard and Judith Polka, the couple who opened that joint to begin with. I was a freshman in high school. I had no friends, nobody to eat lunch with, nobody to do homework with, and no one to gossip with. I remember this one time, it was like the first day of high school I think.

I was so awkward because everyone had someone to sit with at lunch, I felt so out of place that I just decided to take my peanut butter and jelly sandwich to the bathroom stall and eat in silence.

I didn't want to be stared at for being the only kid without friends. But that plan didn't work too well. I guess lunch hour was the time that the janitors cleaned the hallway bathrooms, so somehow I got locked in, of course.

So I sat on the floor just banging on the door but no one came to rescue me for about an hour. Man, that was embarrassing to have to explain to my teacher as to why I was late to class.

Never skipped lunch again after that. But despite that, I still really enjoyed going to school cause it meant I got to get away from my "dad" for eight hours a day, and it made me feel like I could really achieve something in life. Probably would've enjoyed it more if I had friends, though. Whatever. I didn't need friends. I just needed *her*. I even remember the day I met her.

MONDAY, APRIL 11TH, 1960

The day I met my first love. I was walking home from school one spring afternoon, just as I always did, when she walked up next to me and started going in the same direction as me. We started to small talk. I guess her parents usually picked her up. They lived out of town or something and some excuse as to why they couldn't come that day. I can't really remember what it was. I'm not sure, and frankly I was just thankful that they hadn't shown—like it was meant for us to meet. I walked a mile in the wrong direction just so I could walk her all the way home safely. We went together for a while, holding hands in the hallway, sitting together at lunch, making small talk about her family and what we both wanted to do with our lives, and what we liked and didn't like. She never rode home with her parents after that day; I walked her to her house everyday after school at three o'clock, until her parents bought her a car of course and she drove me home.

I guess the moment I fell for her was when she asked me to talk about it. About my past. And it wasn't so much that I was scared of talking about it, but rather being scared of hurting her. She told me it was okay and that she was there for me. I believed her. My voice began to shake. Right there, sitting next to her on a tree stump outside the schoolyard, I started to realize that the pain of every moment I'd been through was worth getting to that moment with her and from that moment on, we were inseparable. Our relationship was deeper than it had been before that conversation, before I fell in love with her. We spent every minute together in the hallways, we would skip lunch and go to the park across the street from our school. She would drive me to work, and we would go to the drive-in movies every Friday night (as long as my Mama didn't need me that night). Her name was Delilah Ann Taylor. She had that kind of curly hair that was so curly it would always stay frizzy. Tall and slender, even slightly taller than me at the time. Light hazel eyes that always seemed as if they were only looking forward.

You could ask her anything and she would tell you the truth, you knew that she would never lie to you. She was that genuine person that everyone wanted to be, and everyone wanted to be with, so happy and carefree. One Friday night, I brought yellow lilies to her at the drive-in and told her how in love with her I was. She reciprocated those feelings and I was the happiest teenager on the planet. It was absolutely perfect... for about five years that is...

It's lights out now, so gotta go.

Graham Embry Soyle
09/08/06

HYACINTHS

Constancy

Tuesday, October 21st, 1969

I **met Bettie in her office after a hard day of work** where she congratulated me on a successful three months of working at the yard. Honestly, it felt like I had been doing it much longer. I was comfortable there. She handed me a thin leather book, maybe 150 pages or so, about flowers.

It was obviously a nonfiction book that contained thousands of flower types, a description of each one, the meaning behind them, different species and colors, how to grow them—you name it, it was in there.

Bettie said she thought I would enjoy it. The pages were definitely worn. I could tell that she spent hours flipping through them and analyzing each aspect of the many different petals.

I grew fascinated with the information as well, for I wasn't the most educated person in the world; I always loved school and wanted to be able to read, write, and speak profoundly.

Perhaps this book opened the doors of education back up for me, because after the discovery of *A Golden Guide: FLOWERS* by Herbert Spencer Zim, I became interested in learning again.

I suddenly wanted to know and memorize every type of flower in existence and read more and more about them. Luckily, I worked at a boneyard, where people delivered different types of flowers everyday to concrete headstones.

Most of the plants that people brought were roses, lilies, tulips, chrysanthemums, and other easy-to-find types. My favorite days were when visitors delivered unique species like the purple hyacinth.

MONDAY, JANUARY 19TH, 1970

The day I happened upon the first bouquet of purple hyacinths I had ever seen. I was digging a hole over by Plot 132 when a man in his 30s walked up to a grave on the left side of me, about four plots away from the one I was digging.

I decided to take a break from work and have a cigarette, because I wanted to give the man some privacy to mourn whoever he was visiting.

I smoked two cigarettes and the man had already left. I slowly walked back over to Plot 132, and kept walking past it to Plot 127: "R.I.P. Martha Elderby, 1942–1970."

There was a beautiful arrangement of flowers; they were

bright purple in color, and the petals seemed to be climbing down the stem as far as they could go in a swirling motion. Reminded me of cake icing.

I rushed to my office and grabbed my flower book from inside the drawer. I had never seen that type of flower before, and I was curious as to what it was called, as well as the meaning behind them. It took me a while to find the hyacinth in my information novel, but there it was.

Belonging to the asparagaceae family, the hyacinth was a plant meant for forgiveness and was often given to individuals as a peace offering of some sort.

Immediately, a little story started in my head as to what Mrs. Elderby's life could have possibly been like and what relationship the middle-aged man had with her.

I came to the conclusion that Mrs. Elderby had been going steady with the man who came to see her, seeing as he didn't stay longer than 10 minutes. That tells me that they didn't know each other all that well.

She may have been battling with depression in regards to another situation, and the only thing that made her happy was her relationship to that man. He probably cheated on her with another woman—younger and more emotionally stable than herself—which sent her over the edge. Literally over the edge, as she probably jumped off of a bridge of some sort and hit a rock below her.

Which would explain the man's reasoning behind delivering purple hyacinths to her gravesite; he felt remorse and guilt over her death and was asking for forgiveness from her in some way.

It was just a guess, but it passed the time. He probably had no idea what that flower really meant. Probably only bought it cause of the beautiful colors.

WEDNESDAY, MAY 15TH, 1968

On my way to the bar, I saw a man sweeping the concrete out front of the abandoned space adjacent to Scott's. I had never met that man before and Meerdin was pretty small, so I wanted to introduce myself. His name was Carl and he said he used to have a chocolate shop there named Coco's Chocolatiers. He told me his wife loved chocolate and was an excellent baker so she made delicious treats for the whole town.

He became sorrowful when bringing up his wife, Coco, so I assumed she had passed away. Never really got the whole story on that one... but I felt bad for him because it looked like he was really trying to keep the empty place clean. It had been on the market for two years already and it never had any passersby stop and glance at it. I thought poor Carl would never sell the joint.

Speaking of chocolate, I'll never forget about this chocolate cake that my Mama used to make on special occasions. The ingredients cost a fair amount of money and Paul despised any sugary substance so she rarely made it, but when it did appear on the kitchen table, I ate every bite as slow as possible so I could savor every delicious, smooth, creamy bite of goodness.

Mama and I would have two or three slices before Paul got home from work, which is when he would toss it upside down into the trash can and yell vulgar words at Mama. Figures.

How could such a bitter, evil man ever enjoy something as sweet and pure as cake?

I have to say I spent most of 1970 glued to the pages of my flower book. It was the sweetest gift anyone had ever given me and I don't know how Bettie knew me so well after so little amount of time.

I knew we had a special connection when she gave me that book. I bought some sticky notes from the convenience store—all different colors and shapes—and strategically planned out what each color was going to be used for. I remember I had flagged the pages that I was already familiar with that particular flower with the neon yellow sticky.

That doesn't mean I never revisited the yellow-marked pages. I certainly did! I used the neon blue color for the pages that I needed to come back to for educational purposes. Blue pages were always the ones I had no knowledge of and wanted to familiarize myself with them incase I saw them in the yard somewhere.

Neon orange stickers were used for all the pages that seemed extra-worn. I figured that those flowers were Bettie's favorites and I wanted to make sure I knew all about those so I could impress her and relate to her about the book. Last but not least were the neon pink stickies.

Every flower page flagged with a pink sticker meant a lot to me. Those were the flowers that spoke to me the most as I was turning the pages, or perhaps flowers I already had a previous connection or history with.

I wouldn't say they were my favorite flowers, but they definitely were special ones. I wish I could tell Bettie how much that book meant to me...

CARNATIONS

ADMIRATION

MONDAY, JULY 21ST, 1969

My first day at the graveyard. There I was standing on top of Meredith Grousher. Well, she was six feet below me in a box but you get the point. I was standing on a dead person. Who knows if she was in heaven, or hell, or if maggots were devouring her innards right then as I stared at her tombstone? Nobody knew, not even Mama knew. Where's Mama? Does Mama even know where she is?

I always wondered: Where does your brain go after you die, and how are we even going to know what we're thinking if we don't actually have a brain to think with? I'd like to believe she is in a better place. A better place than the ranch. A better place than six feet underneath the ground. But to tell you the truth, I have no clue where she is.

I fled the scene so fast and didn't stick around to see whether or not she was buried, cremated, washed away at sea, ripped apart and used as a science experiment... Hell, she could be alive for all I know. Her twisted neck on the kitchen flooring tells me otherwise, but the point is that I wasn't there to say goodbye to her.

Her own son just left her behind without looking back. I wasn't there to pass her on to her afterlife, or whatever it may be. How can someone claim to be so great and mighty, but then put a man like my father on this Earth? I'm sure he's sitting in hell right now. Or I hope he is. I hope that God exists just for that one reason, just so that I know Paul Soyle is burning below my feet right now.

And I don't know who Meredith is but it seems like she had a decent life cause she's got a tombstone and everything. Her family cared enough about her to come to the funeral and say goodbye. I will never forgive myself for leaving Mama there on that cold floor, with only the thoughts in my head telling her I loved her. If only I would have said it out loud one last time, maybe it would've changed things. Maybe she would have heard me.

SUNDAY, AUGUST 17TH, 1969

I remember this day was my first time bonding with Vern. He scared me at first, with his mysterious demeanor and crooked walk. He walked me around the yard and showed me some of his favorite spots, like the low-hanging tree in the corner by his shed and the moss covered stack of rocks in between two of the gravestones. He told me about all the different people he'd seen pass through over the years and how much he started to appreciate life after being surrounded by death all day long. He was wise and served as a grandfather-like figure to me. His views on life began to resonate with me and I enjoyed seeing him often at work. He was nice to have around. He had remnants of jet black hair sprinkled with gray so I wondered if my hair would look kinda like that when I got to be his age.

Back to my first day on the job: I measured six feet with my shovel from the end of Meredith's plot, and jammed the dull thing into the warm, soft earth. I started digging, and for some reason, I imagined I was digging my own grave.

I wanted everything to be perfect for whoever was going to spend eternity there. Damn, now I wish it was me. I wish I was down deep in the earth, away from this terrible box. What I wouldn't give to be anywhere but here. I didn't know who was going to be buried in that hole, but whoever it was deserved to have comfortable quarters. So I made damn sure that the hole was exactly 8 x 3 x 6 feet and that every line was crisp and straight.

I wanted to draw little images on the walls of this person's new home, just with my finger, in the dirt, but I was terrified I wouldn't be able to get out once I jumped in. So I just covered the grave up with a tarp like Bettie told me to do.

I guess we did that in case a thunderstorm came rolling through the night before the poor fellow got the chance to tour his new home. Wouldn't want a house that's flooded right when ya get there, would ya?

I decided I would dig the other grave a few hours later

because I was hotter than a camel in the middle of a desert. I had already filled my water gallon up three times now, and was working on my fourth when I decided to sit on the edge of the yard to take a smoke break and watch Gene run around.

He loved that graveyard. So much grass for him to roll around and play on. I'm not sure he knew who he was playing on, but that was fine. At least one of us could be happy and carefree. Let him be innocent for the time that he had. Vern loved playing with Gene as well and that kept the both of them entertained. After only ash was left of my Doval, I decided to start raking.

There weren't a lot of leaves in the yard, for it was still springtime, but I raked what I could find and made the graveyard look as put-together as I could. I wanted Ms. Murphy to be pleased with my work. After all, she put a lot of trust in me for only meeting me one time. Okay, grave number two: where was it going to be? Let's just say Row 8 Plot 72. Hell, I can't remember everything. Six feet to the right, and there I was. In between a Mr. Eugene Knoble, and a Mr. James Winceton. I wondered who these people were, and whose grave was about to be dug. Maybe it's Eugene's spouse, or James' oldest child? It could be a random individual with no connection to Eugene or James. I'm so curious about other people's lives, probably because nothing good ever happened to mine.

WEDNESDAY, JANUARY 11TH, 1961

The day I tried to kill myself. Or that's what people told me anyway... I mean I was only 14 years old so I really don't remember if it was a thought-out process or just an accident.

Knowing me, probably not a coincidence though. When I was young, I was diagnosed with hyperkinetic reaction of childhood. I guess these days they call it Attention Deficit Disorder (ADD). Then there was manic depression. Shit, they even thought I had Schizophrenia at one point.

If you want my opinion on the matter, then I will tell you that I don't believe in any of the bullshit. If I had kids of my own, I never would've let some fat guy in a white coat with the initials "MD" on his nametag tell me MY kid had any sort of problem. Your kid doesn't have AD-fuckin' D. He's just hyper. Your kid doesn't have "bipolar disorder" either... he's just pissed off that you wouldn't let him have a Hershey bar at the store and then he forgot about it the next moment. And he definitely doesn't have Aspergers or Schizophrenia or something else... he just has an imagination.

Well anyways, my parents didn't have the same clear mind that I have and they were persuaded by Dr. Veremchuk that I had all sorts of issues, and of course, needed to be medicated for it all. If someone dies, there's probably a reason for it. It isn't natural for someone to take compounded powder matter to make them live a little longer. Everybody's just prolonging the inevitable.

Here is an idea for future mankind: Don't take any drugs and follow the natural course of life and die if you're supposed to die and live if you're supposed to live. The end. Quote me on that shit later, please.

Ok back to me killing myself... so I was on a bunch of drugs at 14 years of age. I still remember 'em all to this day. Here's the list:

Meprobamate 200mg: Take 1 tablet by mouth after each meal
Chlorpromazine 200mg: Take 2 tablets by mouth once a day
Chlordiazepoxide 25mg: Take 1 tablet by mouth in the morning and 1 tablet in the evening
Hydralazine 10mg: Take 1 tablet by mouth twice a day

It increased or decreased every month or so. Needless to say, my life was awful. I might have accidentally taken every pill from every prescription bottle I had while Mama was out tending the garden one day. The only thing I really remember is hearing Mama bent over my body that was on the floor of our bathroom, screaming my name and shaking me. I lived, unfortunately. I woke up in the hospital.

But after that, they put me on *even more* medication. Strange, right? From then on, I just pretended to take my pills everyday, when really I just had this mason jar stashed in the yard somewhere that I hid them in everyday.

Alright, time to finish that chore list... Just as I would finish mowing, it seemed like it was already time to mow again. There was so much grass out there... Once I'd finish with one side it was like the other side had already grown again! I'm fairly certain cutting grass took up 70 percent of the time I spent at that cemetery.

I remember the sun was setting in the background when I finally began on my second grave for the day. Bettie came out to check on me and burst into a mischievous cackle. I was lying in my partially dug hole—wheezing—barely able to lift my arms. Bettie politely told me that the job was mine if I wanted it and that I could finish the rest the next day. I guess she saw something in me that no one else ever had. She had faith in me. Pretty sure she was ready to pass it on to somebody. She was getting up there in age, and it was clear to me that she didn't want many responsibilities any more. Man, would I have loved to have a place other than my shitty apartment to call my own. I could do whatever I wanted there; Gene and I could do whatever we wanted there...

Well, I owned a car once in my life... A shitty car. I guess I could've called that my own. It was a hand-me-down though, so I guess I didn't actually own it, but whatever. I remember so clearly the day that I left. I took my little red truck that my Mama passed down to me in 1965—when I was 18— and just started driving north.

I knew I didn't want to go west because that's where all the rich people lived, and obviously I didn't see myself starting a new life anywhere near the Pacific Ocean. I wanted to travel as far away from that ranch as I possibly could. I had a good amount of money saved up from working at this quaint grocery store in town, "Bo-Nansas"—almost everyday after school. It was the only place around that would make an exception to hire at the age of 14, and I worked there for a good four years before leaving, so I had a while to save up. Never really had anything else to spend money on besides snacks to take to school and of course the one pack of Dovals I would pay someone to buy for me a week. I took seven dollars that I found in my father's wallet and the one photo I had with my mother, and I was out the door forever.

I would just sleep in my car when I got tired of driving because I didn't want to spend any more money than I had to. It was kind of nice actually. Driving that far, alone. If I remember correctly it was about 1,200 miles or something? So much time to think about things, so much freedom—the first time I had ever had real freedom before. I had never been out of Topeka. I grew up there and never got a chance to really go anywhere.

So it was liberating to see all the different places, even if just through the windows of my car. The toughest part about that long drive was the feeling I had the whole way. The terrible feeling set in that I didn't have a mother anymore. And I never had a father really.

I had nobody. I would get lost in thought at every single traffic light, which wasn't many since I spent most of my time on the highway, and then I'd get jolted back to reality every time a car honked behind me. Every place I stopped at to refuel, the owners would always ask where I was headed, and I had the same answer every time: Canada.

Not sure why I went with that. It just seemed the farthest away. The awful truth was that I had no fucking clue where I was going or what I was doing. I was a 19-year-old kid with blood on his hands, $1,819 to his name, a truck that shockingly made it as far as it did, no family, no friends, no lover, no home, no job, and no life. Damn, what was I thinking?

MONDAY, SEPTEMBER 20TH, 1967

My favorite part about that drive was driving through Illinois; I had always wanted to go to Chicago. Always heard people talking about it on the television. Man were they right; that place was amazing! Would have just stayed there but I knew it'd be too expensive. Besides, I didn't quite feel far enough away yet, so after a day of exploring the place I got back on the road.

Had some damn good deep dish pizza at Uno's Pizzeria, which would still have to be my favorite food to this day. I would kill for a slice of plain pizza right now, ya know, with just the cheese. If you can get a good cheese pizza then you honestly don't need any toppings.

Despite the wonderful flavor of my dinner that night, I remember making the decision that I was going to continue on with my roadtrip. The people in that city were sort of rude, so I more than likely wouldn't have enjoyed living there. Not that I care to talk to anyone anyway, but I'm also just not used to being in a big city as it is, so I guess I wanted to find another small town to settle down into. Although now that I'm thinking about it, I should've stayed in Chicago... definitely would've stayed out of trouble.

WEDNESDAY, SEPTEMBER 22ND, 1967

A terrible day on my long journey because Louis, my car, broke down. I wound up in some town called Meerdin, which was in Delaware. I don't know much about cars so I don't quite remember what caused it to break down that day. I just remember some nice people around my age pulled up beside me and offered to drive me to an auto shop down the road.

They eventually towed my truck there and fixed whatever needed to be settled with it. Transmission or something like that. Now that was a good chunk of my life savings, but it had to be done. After that happened I thought I'd stick around for a little bit to save money. After all, I had no idea where I was headed anyway; it could've been destiny that my car broke down in Meerdin.

Anyways, I decided to walk into the gas station next door and ask where I could find a decent place to eat. The guy at the counter had suggested a place not too far into town. He said it was really popular amongst the locals and such. It's actually where I found the flyer with the details of that studio apartment off of McCormick Ave that I lived in. It was posted on the bathroom wall of the restaurant: Sal's Patties. At first, you walk up to this little brick-colored joint with a white barn-looking door. There were a bunch of yellow carnations all around the lining of the building. Come to find out the owner's wife planted them every year in remembrance of her grandparents. You could sit on the benches out front, but you just couldn't get anything ordered out there. There were only four spots for people to park. The rest were just first come, first serve for the small amount of grassed area.

Now, walking inside, it had that homey kind of feeling to it. Small faint yellow-colored stools around the main eating area. The rest were leather matching colored booths. The colors of the floors were a mix between relish and an unpeeled lime. Oh, and we can't forget the incredible jukebox towards the back where I would spend my spare change. My go-to song to play was called "Crazy He Calls Me" by the great Billie Holiday. That was my Mama's most cherished song.

I think it might have been how she once felt about my father and never wanted to let go of that feeling. I think it took her back to before, so it was nice to hear it play every now and again when someone selected it. The menu had a lot on it.

Mostly though, just a bunch of different types of burgers. The rest was just breakfast entrees. Glad I took that guy's suggestion; it became my favorite place to go grab a burger. So simple and delicious.

Took about a good two months of me going there before Dawn, the regular waitress, finally remembered my order without me having to specify "no ketchup, please." I don't like ketchup because it reminds me of the many blood stains in the kitchen sink from when my Mama would have to wash off her face after that asshole had another drunken altercation with her. Anyway, the first day I went there, I found that flyer, and went later on that afternoon to look at the place. It was about two miles from Sal's and after slipping the real estate agent a 20 dollar bill to bump me to the top of the list, I was signing the papers to move in within an hour. The complex was called Clover Apartments. They had bigger apartments there but the studio was good enough for me at the time.

Anyway, whenever Bettie told me I got the job, I was ecstatic, because I could see myself in the future. Having something else to call my own. We grew closer and closer throughout the many days of hard work. For the first few months or so, she would meet me at the gates: 8 AM sharp, and write a list of chores that she wanted me to complete for that day. It was pretty generic: ya know, dig "blank" (if any) number of graves, mow the grass, rake, water the flowers, feed the stray cats, lock up, etc.

Usually, Ms. Murphy would just sit in her tiny, brick, 10 x 10-foot cube of an office building that was positioned on the back left corner of the graveyard in front of Vern's house, all day. She'd watch me from behind her electric fan for hours.

She would watch me through the window. Not because she was really checking up on me, or even because she was bored, but because I think she saw me as the son she never had. She would always make me come in and sit with her every hour or so and talk.

Not like she really had anything to talk to me about. She hadn't really had anything happen to her in her lifetime. Other than Murphy Creek, she didn't have anything else. She usually shared her tuna sandwich and pickle with me for lunch and everyday was pretty much the same. Some days there were no graves to dig at all, and those were the days that Bettie and I really talked about our lives.

Sometimes Vern would stagger over as well and join in on the conversation. He used a baseball bat as a cane, so he had a bit of a hunchback, but surprisingly it worked pretty well for him. I remember Bettie telling me that her parents were both born and raised in Meerdin, that they were friends for most of their lives, and married at the age of 18 in 1918.

One year later, they gave birth to the great Bettie Lynn Murphy. Ms. Bettie claimed that she was a rebel teenager. I guess she disobeyed her parents a lot and started smoking at the age of 12, but I think most people did back then. Her previous relationships weren't always her favorite topic to discuss so she didn't talk about that much, but when she did, I got the impression that she was a bit of a floozy. Ya know, pretty sure she was on a different man's arm every other night or so. But I was never one to judge. I just accepted her for who she was, no matter what life she may have lived; she was my boss, my friend, and a wonderful motherly figure for me to admire. I remember this particular day quite vividly; it was a Thursday morning in November of '68. Ms. Bettie and I had just opened the gates and stepped inside her office to look at the daily chores when I spotted this old man out the window. I had seen him before. He would come once a week—for an hour or two—always on Thursday. But on this particular Thursday, he came and stayed from open to close, standing there raking leaves off of a plot, just talking to the headstone. There weren't any graves to be dug that day and it hadn't rained in a couple days so I didn't really need to cut the grass. Therefore, we just watched this man the whole time. He probably thought he was alone in that graveyard, and we wanted to keep it that way so we made sure we stayed out of sight, which was hard cause Gene kept trying to scurry through the hole at the bottom of the door.

We wanted to let the man raking leaves have his moment with the lost individual. At one point he took out food that he had in his backpack. Maybe he was having a picnic with who I assumed was his wife. I had never actually gone over to find out what the stone said, but that day struck my curiosity. Once I finished my shift, I walked over to see who he was visiting only to notice the gravestone read "R.I.P. Agatha." I made a story up in my head over the following weeks of who Agatha and this Thursday Man were, and how much he loved her, and how happy they were together.

He looked like he was in his early 70s, so I assume Agatha was around the same age. I bet they met before the war, and fell in love, got married around '41 before he was shipped off to war. I could picture them having kids when the war ended and living life to the fullest until she died from cancer of some sort. Not the best life, but it seemed like a pretty acceptable life to me. Wish my parents could have been that way, ya know, just live and die a normal life. I named him Doug just to make his visits more memorable to me, but I never saw him after that day. I watched him every afternoon for a month until one day I had the chore of digging a hole right next to Agatha's plot, and I couldn't help but think that it was Doug's new home.

TUESDAY, OCTOBER 6TH, 1970

One of my most fond memories of Bettie was in the afternoon. It was a typical tuna and pickles, the exact lunch where she finally got up the urge to tell me about her one and only true love; Walter Chase. The way she spoke of him, you could just tell how much she cherished him. Her eyes dilated as soon as she said his name. It made me think of Delilah. To spend so much of your life feeling that way about one person, I knew how Bettie felt.

Ya know you just love someone so much you become one soul. But she had years on me, plenty more years of wisdom than I had had at the time to think day in and day out about the same person. I couldn't imagine such loyalty to a person, especially being loyal to someone you can't even be with, but she was the most loyal person I ever knew.

There we were in her office and she just started talking and talking… "I was around 18 years young, no real obligations other than helping my parents tend to the family graveyard. I had just graduated school and my mother and father didn't have the finances to send me away to university. They did, however, save up a few hundred dollars for me, which allowed me to go on a weekend trip to New York City with a few of my girlfriends. It was our last night in the city and my friends sent me out to the market to try to get alcohol. I suppose I did look the oldest with my curly blonde hair, green eyes, thin figure, and larger-than-average sized bust. I was young and free. I loved my life and saw no need for change at the moment.

But when I walked out into that market, there he stood, leaning against the brick wall. I'll never forget the color of his stained brown boots or the dust in his hair. He was just drinking a Coca-Cola and staring off into space. I could see the beads of sweat rolling down his cheek from being in that thick tan uniform all day. Then our eyes met.

It was an instant connection. He went from leaning to standing straight up in a matter of seconds and I was able to talk to him. He was tall and fit, with dark brown hair that was slicked to the left side, dimples on both cheeks, and charcoal gray eyes. From that moment on my life changed. He was on leave for two more weeks after meeting him at the grocer's that day, and those 14 consecutive days would be known as the best days of my life. I didn't leave with my friends that next day to go home, for instead I decided to see where this new interest went.

Walter happened to be from the city, and was on leave from flying with the United States Army Air Corps. We fell in love quickly and hard that June, talking about our lives and our families. I even met his family, saw a play together, ate hot dogs at Coney Island, talked about our future. We ended up getting married on a whim when he was home for a few days on leave, and even though it was spontaneous, that man had a wonderful ring already picked out and ready for me. Every waking moment that he wasn't away we were in each other's arms. He was gone a lot though; the military does that to a person. It was hard sometimes but it was worth it.

You would never believe how much closer you get to a person when you're apart for so long, Graham. We would go months and months only being able to write letters to each other, but the joy of walking to the mailbox and seeing that envelope with his handwriting on it... it was the best feeling in the world.

I was never even able to make it five feet away from the mailbox before tearing it open so I could start to imagine his voice talking to me. Every letter I read from him I cried from happiness that we were one day closer to being together again. He would always end his letters with 'yours completely, Wally.'

That was the nickname I had given him. Wally was perfect, we were perfect. Until the plane crash he got into in 1945 of course. Almost five years of writing letters back and forth, seeing each other for days at a time, weeks at a time at most.

That darn plane crash was the catastrophe that ended our fairy tale. I'll never forget when we made the commitment to finally buy our own place. It was real. We were going to be to-gether forever.

I remember opening up my brown, rickety front door to two men dressed in uniform. That's when I knew that forever wasn't forever anymore. One told me the bad news in the most scholarly, sophisticated tone, as he passed me the very last letter Walter ever wrote to me, while the other one caught me in his arms as I fell to the ground in devastation, squalling. I guess he never had the chance to mail it before he went up in the air. But a single woman I've been since. If Wally can't hold my heart, nobody can."

WEDNESDAY, OCTOBER 7TH, 1970

My absolute worst memory of Bettie. I walked into Sal's that night, not knowing what to think or what to do. "What's gonna happen with my job? What's gonna happen with the graveyard? Am I going to have to bury her in her own cemetery?" were the only thoughts running through my brain at the time. I thought maybe if I just sat down and ate and sobbed into my burger, that it would make me suddenly have the answers to all of these questions. But all it did was make me have more questions. I didn't know how the hell I was going to afford rent or food for Gene or flowers for Bettie with no job and no money coming in.

After ordering a cheeseburger and a water, Dawn realized that I was distressed and she sat down next to me at the bar. After explaining to her what had happened to my friend, my boss, my second mother, she left me to eat my burger in peace, along with sliding a complimentary beer to me across the bar. I took my time, too.

Dawn actually told me I had to leave around 10:55 PM because they were about to close. She told me it was on the house that night; I guess cause she still felt sympathy for me. She turned around and walked back to the kitchen to finish up the dishes for that night, and suddenly I had the idea. The genius idea that I'm sure led me to where I am today somehow. On every table in Sal's sat a small cup with three carnations in them. All of them were white. I guess the owner brought some from his wife's garden out front and placed them around the restaurant to add to the fun atmosphere already in place there.

My idea was to take the carnations from Sal's that night: 1) because it seemed as if they were giving away everything else for free that night, so why not the flowers, too? 2) because I woke up that morning with no job and no expectations of being able to keep the graveyard, so officially I was unemployed. 3) I really needed flowers to bring to Bettie's remembrance service the next day, and I had no time to travel to the only flower shop outside of town, nor did I have money to pay for the flowers.

So I did it. I snatched the three carnations that were placed on one of the tables and rushed out the front doors of the restaurant. I then stopped by the garden of carnations out front and plucked nine more. Flowers in groups of three rubbed me the wrong way. Besides, Bettie deserved a whole dozen.

Graham Embry Soyle
09/20/06

ORCHID

Love, Luxury, Beauty, and Strength

My Dearest Graham,

    I know this might come as a heartache to you, but, I leave you today, with only three keys. There are some deeper things that I never really got around to telling you about. I, a lot of the time, struggle with harsh depression. I always have. Just the thought of having lost my Wally, it becomes very hard to cope with a lot of the time. I'm sure it's difficult for you to understand. You're still young, but one day, you will.

    There comes a time in one's life where you find even the thought of being alive to be so unbearable that you no longer want to exist. Being in a world without the love of your life, well, it isn't much of a life at all and I've dealt with it for far too long now. I hope that every day, maybe, just maybe, I would be happy again. It's hard to go through your day-to-day activities having to pretend that someone is there with you when they're not.

And that's what I've had to do, year in and year out. I wake up every morning, having my breakfast with a second cup of coffee in front of me, just imagining he is there with me. From there I find myself stuck in the same depressing place that's been haunting me since my childhood: the graveyard. Where I see people's hearts destroyed as they bury their loved ones.

It's like I'm finding out Walter passed away all over again, every time. It's heartbreaking. I just can't do it any longer. I probably would have gone through with this a long time ago if it wasn't for you taking an interest in myself and my graves. I truly loved spending the days with you in my office and sharing moments passed with you over spoiled tuna, stale crackers, and pickles. It let me hold on to life for a little bit longer. After sharing that story with you today about Walter I thought, and I realized I will never fully be able to let go of my love or my sorrow.

And so I regret to express to you that I have decided to take my life away from yourself and the good ole city of Meerdin, in hopes that I will find Walter.

I know they won't find me, so I am going to tell you what my plan is so that you aren't just sitting around wondering what ever happened to me, but I would prefer that nobody else knows, so please just leave me down there.

I plan, tonight, to go to the Pond of Wishes, and ask God to take me to my Wally. To finally bring me back to the happiness I have longed for. To take away my sadness and sorrows. I plan to tie a brick to my weak body with an orchid in my pocket and walk until I cannot stand and let life take me to where I am supposed to be. Orchids represent everything I wish to bring with me into the afterlife, so hopefully the presence of one during my death will bring good fortune to me. I know you understand the importance of flowers better than anyone I know.

I can imagine you're feeling some sort of hate towards me right now, wondering why I would choose to tell you these things. I am sorry, only for the reason that I let you become so close to me. But I am not sorry that we became close. You were the first person since Walter that I ever even gave the time of the day. You have been the only person who has truly cared for me and spent time trying to get to know me. And you will never know how much that meant to me.

Although, in thoughts of trying to explain myself, I have chosen to leave everything I have to you. That includes the key to Meer Murphy Creek, the key to my house on Farghue Lane, and the key to the locked toolbox in the shed, which holds my life savings.

I know none of this makes up for my leaving you, but it's a decent start, I think. I do hope you do good things with what I've left to you. I do hope you find your true happiness. I hope you get far with your future endeavors.

Yours Completely, Bettie

FRIDAY, OCTOBER 9TH, 1970

Was hard. Going to Bettie's remembrance service reminded me of the funeral that I did not attend. No, I do not mean my mother's. I'm not even sure if she had one. I'm talking about my one true love, Delilah. God, do I miss her still to this day. I regret almost every day of my life not going to her funeral.

What a selfish ass I was. Correction. What a selfish ass I am. The one chance I had to see her for the last time and I threw it away. I am so fucking stupid. I am so worthless. Suppose I don't blame Bettie. Sometimes I feel the same way she felt.

Almost every day I pretend that Del is here with me. I sometimes talk to her while I'm eating my dinner. It beats talking to the concrete wall. I used to talk to her on my evening walks when I lived in Meerdin, but then Gene took her place.

Gene helped me a lot honestly: kept me company, especially after Bettie was gone. But it's still not the same, ya know. He couldn't ever talk back to me, no matter how much I wished he could. He could never help me with my problems, or hold me at night when I had outlandish dreams. No matter how much I wanted a companion to hold at night, unfortunately Gene couldn't serve as that type of companion. I remember this one time, it was Del's birthday or perhaps it was Valentine's Day.

Either way, I had taken her to one of my favorite places. It was a field that I hadn't shown anyone before. It was called Rednevalley Field, one of the most beautiful places I had ever seen. It was just a random two acres or so of land that was enclosed by a bright red wood fence. Inside the fence was thousands and thousands of planted lavender. Not only was lavender Delilah's favorite color, but I thought showing her the field would allow her into my heart a little bit more. And it worked, too. She loved it.

We laid there for hours just holding hands and talking, looking up at the disfigured clouds. It was one of the better days of my whole life. Certainly one I could never forget.

Nevertheless, the day of Bettie's initial service is one I'll remember as well. I took the carnations to Ms. Bettie's "grave" that day. They were white, ya know, the ones from Sal's garden. She was always pointing that color out to me, so I think it may have been one of her favorites. I watched from the sidelines during the ceremony because I was terrified of being forced to make a speech, and then I went over to pay my respects after everyone left. Well, after the four people that were there left.

Let's see, there was Dawn, from Sal's. There was Abby, from the market Bettie went to. Vern, of course, was there. And then there was Ingrid, who I hadn't seen since my paperboy days. Bettie didn't really talk much to anyone. But at least she had a few people that cared enough about her to show up and remember her for the wonderful person that she was. I think people knew that she was never going to turn up, that she was dead somewhere.

See, Bettie's case was treated as a missing person's case. She wasn't considered legally "dead" until the seventh year of being MIA. Therefore, we couldn't have a funeral service for her until October 9th, 1977. The funeral wasn't much different from the remembrance service seven years before. Same people, same place, same atmosphere. I remember feeling strange, because the funeral was an empty-casket ceremony.

The detectives never did find Bettie's body. However, I knew where her body lay, so I felt like I was committing a crime of some sort, which I was. I could've told the police where her body was back in 1970 and given her the proper burial when she was supposed to have it, but she wanted it that way. She didn't want anybody to find her, so I kept my promise for my whole life.

Until now, of course. This is my journal of secrets. This is my journal of thoughts, but they aren't thoughts. They are memories. Whoever is reading this, know that everything is true. For better or for worse, I can't hold my stories in anymore, they must be let out. I am truly sorry. Alas, the four individuals at the funeral left, and even though I knew Bettie wasn't under the ground—that we were pretending she was— I still said a few words to her and left my dozen white flowers for her. I still miss her to this day. Luckily, the police investigation wasn't as thorough as it could've been. Her property couldn't be claimed by the government until she was deceased, so I managed to keep access to her three keys, until the seventh year of her being missing passed, unless I had revealed the paper she wrote to me stating that I owned everything... but obviously I never did that.

THURSDAY, APRIL 19TH, 1962

Remember that cow that I mentioned a while ago? The one I got when I was eight years old on my birthday. Betsy! My beloved, big, beautiful Betsy! Well, she loved fields. I mainly wanted a cow as a present because I knew it's about the only thing I would be able to have. I thought a cow could provide service to my father by giving milk to him, and could provide service to me in the form of being a friend.

I didn't know anybody out there in Kansas in the middle of nowhere, and I was too young to leave and explore. So, when I got that cow for my birthday, I felt true joy. I spent every waking moment with Betsy. I would walk with her around the ranch all day and talk to her about the weather and my daily chores.

She was so attentive, sometimes I thought she said things back to me. But perhaps that was just my imagination running wild as it always has. I took her on walks through the grass fields behind the ranch house, because she loved the tall blades of grass and weeds that would rub against her black and white leathery skin.

One day in April, when I was about 15, I took her on a typical walk behind the house, and this day I will never forget. It's like a switch flipped in my skull... something snapped inside of me... I had never before felt such rage until that very moment on that breezy Thursday morning. Betsy was wandering a few feet in front of me, moving slowly through the leaves, when she stopped for a moment, bent her short neck down towards the ground, sniffed a flower, and then slammed her mouth down on a daisy and ripped it right out of the earth, root and all.

She looked so happy eating that fucking daisy... I could just see the white petals being destroyed in between her teeth. Something hit me; a dark cloud floated above me, an evil switch in my brain turned on, my sinister side came through the darkness and into the light, and I couldn't handle it. I couldn't breathe. Even thinking about it now, I'm getting mad. It's like, how can you stand there on all fours with your black and white ass and enjoy a daisy in front of me like that. What courage Betsy had... the nerve she had to do that.

My face turned purple, my teeth and fists clenched together tight, I swung the right ball of knuckles towards her smooth body, jamming my fist into her side. I kept swinging at her. I couldn't stop myself. Even after I heard poor Betsy cry out, I couldn't stop. I hit harder and harder, I wanted her to fall over. I wanted her to suffer for enjoying a meal like that, in front of me. The only thing I remember after that was being pulled off of Betsy by my Mama, who in turn, slapped me across the face in disgust.

She was mortified, and so was I. I felt horrible afterwards, and the worst part is I had nothing to explain my horrific actions that night. I lost a dear friend that day... Betsy never trusted me again.

I'm not sure that my Mama ever wanted to forgive me for that either. I mean why would she? I can't even imagine the disappointment she must have felt that night. She kept asking me why I did it, and I think I subconsciously knew. It just hadn't registered in my brain quite yet.

Shortly after that on the following Monday, I was in Algebra class when my teacher got a call from the guidance office downstairs, asking for me! I always got nervous when the phone rang because nothing ever good happened to the kids summoned to the office.

The whole class booed and laughed when I left the classroom, as if I just lost a talent show or something. Turns out it wasn't as bad as I thought: I guess my Mama was worried about my wellbeing and asked the counselor if he would try talking to me. Ha. Like that worked. But I went along with it for a little while. I think I saw Mr. Cables every Monday for about two months before class.

We never really talked about anything serious. I only kept going because he was, sadly, the closest thing I had to a friend. I think it made my Mama happy that I had *someone* to talk to though. After that incident with Betsy, I never harmed another animal, so I guess counseling did something for my little messed up brain. Animals are so innocent...poor girl didn't deserve what I did to her. She had no idea what she was doing.

Hell, I hardly even knew why it upset me, so how could

she? I don't have too many regrets, but my big ole Betsy is certainly one of them.

MONDAY, SEPTEMBER 25TH, 2006

The current day. I don't have to look at a clock to know what time it is anymore. I can feel each and every hour rushing across the world, plus I have this new mouse friend and he happens to run around at the same stroke of midnight, every night.

Well so I guess that means it's actually the 26th now. But tonight I just happened to wake up cause I can't stay asleep when laying on this DAMN CARDBOARD! So I guess I'll share some of my thoughts with you until I feel tired again. I'm writing in the dark just so you know...Let's talk about September 17th. It is my least favorite day of the year, of any year. Ya see, it's the day I was born, the day I was brought into this terrible world, back in 1946.

That's not why I hate the day though. The 17th of September is also the date I share with my Mama's death. That's the day my father finally beat her to death.

Yes, you read that right... my Mama was murdered by her own husband, my father, Paul Richard Soyle, on my 21st birthday in 1967. So my birthday every year isn't exactly one that I want to think about.

I remember when Ms. Bettie brought me a slice of chocolate cake to share in the office in September of '69 for my 23rd birthday. It was a chocolate-iced, chocolate cake with fudge on the inside, too. Gosh it was so much chocolate... but it was sweet of her to do that, pretty sure that was the last time I had any kind of sweets given to me on my birthday since. Which is fine, it was a good memory. I still miss her quite a lot.

I can't even remember if I told Bettie about my Mama or not. But that's the past anyway, I wouldn't want her to be even more disappointed in me anyway. Now that I've upset myself, I'm going back to sleep. Night.

Thursday, September 28th, 2006

Today. My dearest apologies for falling asleep the other night before finishing my story. I was attempting to tell you some of the better memories of my life. Most of my stories in this journal are all dark and depressing, like my soul, but all people have some blissful experiences in life so let me share one of mine with you.

That chocolate-iced, chocolate cake was sensational. I was so happy that someone had actually remembered my birthday, that I forgot to even say thank you for the cake. My birthday in 1961 was a good one, too. I turned 15 that day, and I lost my virginity to Delilah. It was so calm and quiet and peaceful; everything just felt right that day.

So it was planned. I even remember what my lovely Del wore that day: it was a light pink and white flower dress. She looked so beautiful, I should have known she was too good to be true. We drove out to our Rednevalley Fields in the middle of that breezy September day, and just did it right there, amongst the field of what used to be beautiful lavender. I told

73

her I would never let anything bad happen to her. Our favorite place to spend our days together. It was so gentle, loving, romantic; it was everything I had ever wanted it to be. Oh, and I can't forget about my birthday a couple weeks ago! That was one of the best ones I've had since I got here. It was macaroni day at lunch! Who doesn't love some macaroni!?

See, I can talk about happy stuff, 'til next time.

Graham Embry Soyle
09/28/06

SUNFLOWERS

Strength and Loyalty

Sunday, October 11th, 1970

The realization hadn't set in yet that I had a business to manage and I had no employees to help me at the time. I mean the graveyard had already been closed for a few days because everything happened way too fast and I had no clue where to start. I decided that one more day wouldn't hurt anything and I hopped on my rusty bicycle with the squeaking handlebars. Sometimes I did miss my delivery routes.

I tied Gene's leash to the right handlebar so he could run next to me and started to pedal. I couldn't get the taste of chamomile tea out of my mouth ever since the funeral. Seeing Ingrid brought back some memories I guess I had forgotten about. Made me realize how much I've missed out on. It was around 9:30 AM, so I knew that Ms. Freya Robbins would be home cause that was the time I usually crossed her path on my route. Upon pulling up to her house, the first detail that caught my eye every time was the hot pink mailbox. It made no sense at all. The majority of the rest of her home was pure white.

That damn mailbox though got me every time. Brightest pink you can imagine, with "Freya Robbins" written in white cursive letters on the side. The box itself wasn't your typical style mailbox. It was a replica of her actual house, the only difference being the color. In the center of the tiny pink French doors were an eight-inch wide slot made for the common letter. I knocked on her porcelain white door twice, and she answered with a smile on her face. She welcomed Gene and I into her home, fetched me a cup of chamomile tea, and sat down in her white velvet chaise.

The inside of Ingrid's home looked like a museum or something. Very modern looking, black and white furniture, crazy looking glass art all over the place, a couple fur rugs laying around, and she had a bird, too. Its bird cage was so big I didn't even feel bad that it was trapped. I was always afraid of dropping my tea and staining the rug or Gene misbehaving and shitting all over the place. Something that could totally happen, especially with my luck.

You could tell this woman had money just from looking at the inside of her house. I never cared about the money though, really. Ingrid was so kind to me, and I felt like I could talk to her about anything, even more than Bettie. I saw Bettie as a motherly figure, and there are definitely certain topics I would never talk about with my Mama, but with Ingrid, I had no problem talking to her about my hardships, or my loves. I would curse in front of her when I needed to and she would listen to whatever I had to say. She even knew stories about my father.

Wednesday, June 17th, 1957

Was one of my only fond memories of my father. When I put aside how he treated my Mama, I realize my childhood wasn't always bad. I remember when I was close to turning 12, my dad took me fishing at this little creek he called "the hole."

I think this was before he started drinking. Times weren't bad until after he started drinking. I wonder what happened with him that he felt the need to start drinking his life away and throw away his marriage and kid?

Anyway, I guess this place was where he and his dad, also named Paul, used to go every other weekend. But I don't remember ever meeting my grandpa. He died when I was really young, and maybe that's why my dad waited so long to show me "their spot." But it was nice, kind of in the middle of nowhere, but so are most jewels in the world when you think about it. There were a lot of trees, frogs, and mosquitoes. I actually felt kind of close to him back then.

That was the first time I had ever caught a fish—a flathead catfish to be exact. It was also the last fish I ever caught. Dad never took me back to "the hole" after that day. I'll never forget the look on his face when I reeled in that five-pound catfish. He was so... proud. It was kind of like the rare times he would play catch with me after school before he went to work. Every time we did play ball, he would make me go a little further back to see if I could throw further that day. I enjoyed the challenge; ended up playing baseball in high school. Well I rode the bench most afternoons but I was still a member of the team. Maybe if I didn't just stop showing up to school I would have gotten a scholarship or something, who knows, but instead I thought I needed to start working so I could help the parents with bills and whatnot.

Regardless, I never got to see him look like that again. Oh well. At least the one thing I learned from him was how not to be. I don't want to be anything like him. I wonder if I'll ever go see my Mama. I wonder who found her. If she's buried or cremated.

Sometimes I regret just disappearing; I mean it was the place I grew up but I just couldn't do it. I couldn't be at that place any more. I guess the only thing I don't regret about leaving was knowing that I was finally putting all the bad behind me, for the time being at least. I just wish I could have saved my Mama, too.

She deserved so much more. She was perfect with her shoulder-length brown hair, light green eyes, caramel skin tone, and the most beautiful smile you'd ever see. She went to church every Wednesday and Sunday, which was probably the happiest time of her week. I'm not really sure how she met my father, or why she didn't leave him. But that's how her life was and she finally paid for it.

Farghue Lane was only a few blocks south of Ingrid's home, so I decided to go check out Bettie's old home/my new home. I had never been to her house before, which surprises me looking back on it. She had no family to clean it out before I got there, so I was nervous to see what secrets she had kept in her house while we knew each other. She could've been an undercover detective for all I knew. Maybe she had a secret office in the basement. Doubtful... but you never know.

There I was. 4432 Farghue Lane, Meerdin, DE, 19907. Narrow cobblestone driveway leading up to a white front door with a ripped screen in front of it. Mailbox was just a generic dirty white stick in the dirt with three numbers on the side: "4," "4," and "2." The "3" must've fallen off sometime before that and Ms. Bettie didn't give a damn to replace it. I respected that a little bit. She didn't care what others thought of her home, as long as she knew what number was missing. She didn't care if anybody else knew.

And guess what? I never replaced that "3" sticker either; it wasn't worth the 50 cents, and if Ms. Bettie didn't care, why should I? There was an old station wagon in the driveway, green paint falling off the side, license plate expired. I didn't even know Bettie had a car, she never drove it to work or even mentioned it, and she didn't give it to me in her will either. The grass in her yard surprisingly wasn't too high. I was surprised to see that she didn't have any flowers planted in the front or the back yard.

I walked up to the entry door and turned the key in the deadbolt. I attempted to open it, but it was locked. So, I turned the key again. Either I was being an idiot as usual, or the front door wasn't even locked when I got there! I guess that's the last thing you think of doing as you leave to go drown yourself in a lake, right? ... "Wait, let me lock the door really quick..."

I walked into a carpeted, small, wallpapered home that smelled like metal and wood shavings. Average size, normal looking house. I did see two cups of coffee on the dining room table though, one full and one empty, just like in her story about Walter.

I found a gun box underneath her bed; the box was open and the gun was gone. She didn't shoot herself, so I'm not sure where she would've put it. The back of her house had a screened-in patio with a couple rusty chairs on it and a run-down shed in the back.

Inside the shed were dozens and dozens of shovels, all of different sizes and conditions. I came back inside to take it all in and sat on her floral-print sofa.

All of a sudden, a terrible feeling rushed over me, and I went back to the last time I sat on a sofa just like that...

THURSDAY, DECEMBER 23RD, 1964

I was just getting off of a 10-hour shift at Bo-Nansas when I came home to some cops sitting in our living room, my Mama's eyes were filled with tears. All I could think was, "What did that bastard do this time?" Until the Sheriff came over to me, putting his hand on my left shoulder, face looking down towards his shoes.

So I shuffled over and sat down next to Mama on our flowered sofa while they told me the worst news I could have ever gotten. I could never really explain to you what exactly I felt in that moment because you would hear nothing but dark thoughts and loud curse words.

There just isn't any way to explain what it feels like to lose your first love out of nowhere, so young. It may have just been another moment in time for those sheriffs, even for Mama, but it changed every single moment that followed for me. But now it's just a series of images that flash through my mind at times that I least expect it, which used to be weekly, but now I flashback to this time about once a year.

Fuck, am I exhausted of remembering that night. I just want it to drift further into my past. I want the memories to fracture and splinter until all I can remember is not a feeling, but a picture. I want to go back to when all the space around me wasn't empty... In those moments of relapse, I am completely empty.

My sweet Delilah had been found by some local neighborhood kids out in a ditch where they played hide n' seek in the dark. They weren't afraid to give me details, but I'll spare you the horror; her body half under an oak tree that had been wiped out by a tornado earlier that year. She had been raped and left naked there to die.

I knew it was him, I just knew it. HE told me he was going to *get me back* for trying to stand up for Mama that one night. HE told me that I would *regret* it. And where was he that night? Nowhere to be found. I couldn't say a word, I could hardly breathe or look at anyone. I had my fists clenched so hard that my fingernails were breaking the skin of my palms. I couldn't figure out if my body was going to burst out in tears or start screaming at the top of my lungs.

Turned out to be neither. I got up and just started running. I ran and ran until my limbs gave out and I was face up in the middle of the street. Only one street light worked on that road, so I doubt anyone driving could have seen me to stop, but at that point I just didn't care.

They never found any prints on her body to lead to anyone, so nothing ended up happening. Her family did have a funeral for her at the land they owned at their ranch, about three miles away from our ranch, which wasn't really that far considering we walked about five miles to school every morning. Though I just couldn't bring myself to show my face.

Sometimes I wish I would have gone but I couldn't help but feel responsible for not protecting her from him. I promised I would never let anything happen to her. How could I break the only promise I ever made to her? From then on I never made a promise again.

I'm not sure that I can ever be happy. I tried for so long. Five years! I'm sure to most people, that's not very long. But to me, obviously it was. It still is. Do people really last that long? Longer? I just don't really know how to be happy.

I wanted so badly to be with her and I wanted so badly to be happy. I wanted so badly to be accepted and I just no longer know what to do anymore. I wanted to love and I wanted to be happy but I cannot have both, and the world has made that very known.

There's no chance of happiness now; I lost my freedom 21 years ago. Should the two stay together because of time? Because of reality? Because of normality? Because of comfort?

No, two should stay together for one reason and one reason only—inseparable love. Love so devoted that one is lost without the other. I can only hope that one day someone will feel something strong enough towards me that they will come to my funeral.

If I even have a funeral. Was recently thinking about getting cremated, but who knows at this point. I wonder if I even get the decision? The guards here will probably just throw me around a bit and then kick me down a sewer to rot.

Monday, October 12th, 1970

Was the fourth day the graveyard had been closed since the incident. It was time to go back to work and figure out how I was going to take over Bettie's duties. I had already made the decision that I wasn't going to hire someone to take my old gravedigging job. I mean, Bettie didn't actually do anything other than sit in her office and tell me the daily orders, so I figured I could manage digging the graves, and running the place at the same time. I also had Vern to help me if I ever did need him. He was always willing to do anything.

I remember when I first came back, Vern came staggering speedily out of his house. He was rushing towards the sound of the gate opening so fast that he forgot to feel around with his makeshift cane and he tripped on a rock and fell down. I ran over to him to make sure he was okay, and he couldn't stop hyperventilating.

He was so concerned as to where I had gone and wanted to make sure I was continuing to run the graveyard. I told him that he could continue living in the house behind the shed. I mean, the guy was blind... I didn't think he would cause any issues for me.

I had some difficulty those first few weeks, not really with completing the daily routine. That part was easy, ya know: open the gates, take the orders down for the number of graves, schedule the funeral procession and burial times, dig said number of graves, rake the leaves and tend to the yard, clean the office, and lock up.

The difficult part was heading into the office at noon to share a tuna sandwich with Bettie, and having her not be there waiting for me. The hard part was looking through the office window from the outside and not seeing her little head peeking through. The worst part of all was looking at Bettie's old desk, and seeing the exact spot right underneath the corner of the desk lamp, where her suicide letter lay that one morning a week or so earlier.

No... even worse than that was having to walk past her plot in the yard every day, multiple times in a day. I knew where her body was. Sometimes I thought I should go get it from the lake and bury her in the hole where she is supposed to be. But then I would've been charged with murder probably and ended up in prison... Go figure. Hah. Prison. That sounds shitty. Oh, wait! It is fucking shitty. Shittier than my fucking shit. Anyways, when I found that letter on her office desk, I didn't know what to do. I didn't know if I should report it to the police, or ignore it, or cry.

So, I took the note and the three keys, filed a missing person's report, explained my story to the police that she wasn't at work that morning, and sat around and waited anxiously for a call or a letter. I heard back from the sheriff that same afternoon and was told that they concluded the case to be a "runaway" case or voluntary disappearance basically. They said I had the ultimate decision as to "wait for her to return home" or to have a funeral service for her. I guess she had listed me in her will as the one to handle all services after death, even though her will contained nothing but that statement. The letter she left me was her will to me though, and I knew that.

Obviously, I had the funeral service because there was no chance of her "coming home" and I didn't want people to suspect anything. Everyday that I walked into that office after her death, my memory shot right back to the moment I discovered the letter. I'll never forget the feeling I had after reading it...so many emotions... I felt honored that she had trusted me with information like that. I felt sad that she was gone, but happy that she was happy. I felt guilty for bringing the conversation up about Walter that ultimately made her decide to end her life.

Most of all, I felt overwhelmed with the sudden death of a friend and the new responsibilities that were thrust upon me all at once. I never forgot about her, but I did learn how to move on.

Tuesday, October 20th, 1970

A chilly afternoon. I hadn't really seen Scotty much since I had been spending so much time at the graveyard. Since Bettie had passed just two weeks before, I'd been trying to keep myself occupied. But on this particular afternoon, I decided to go have a drink with him.

He seemed pretty much the same. We took our shot of Scotch, and instead of leaving after one, I thought I would order a real drink. So I went with a rum and Coke, also known as the "Cuba Libre." Seemed to be the popular choice for most of the guys in there.

We just spent the hours catching up and before I left he

actually invited me to come meet his girlfriend that I suppose he had had for a while.

They were going to the drive-in later that night so I thought it might be good for me to join, to actually have some social interaction for once in my life. So I did. The only option that night was *Carrie*, a horror film.

Which was fine with me. I liked the idea of a movie screen attempting to scare me. Though it failed at the attempt to make me scream or jump, I did enjoy being out with people and doing something aside from my ritual walk, smoke, and Little Kings. Although, I did bring a six-pack with me to the movie to keep my buzz going.

Scott and his girlfriend, Christina, seemed good together, very affectionate. But that's to be assumed in a fairly new rela-tionship. I was happy for them. That they found one another. Slightly jealous. I mean she was beautiful—with that long straight black hair, so dark that it had just the slightest blue tint, gorgeous hourglass body, and a laugh that was simply in-toxicating.

I tried so hard all night to keep my eyes from wandering in her direction, though almost impossible not to. I always saw Scott as a, I don't know, nerdy type of guy. He was tall and lanky, with scruffy, dirty blonde hair and he had one of those beards that don't actually count as a beard because it's too patchy. He sort of had a squeaky voice, too.

How did he manage to catch this woman? I never found out. I was always hopeful that one day I would find someone who would, for some reason, fall in love with me. I'm still hopeful. I doubt there is another; I was already lucky enough to experience it once. Not sure I even want it again. How could anyone else accept me as I am? I always loved thinking about the fairy-tale marriage that Walter and Bettie had, but then again, being married is being able to know that there is that person who wants your particular version of you. It's easier to ignore everything when you think that no one else is out there; it's easier to go day by day without worrying.

I'm not going to put a date on this one, because these memories are occurring right now. I just want to talk to you, as I am today. Sometimes I feel remorse for the things that I've done, but then other times, I really don't care. Actually, most of me doesn't give a shit at all. I was simply trying to make myself sound human, but let's face it, I'm not. I am very far from any type of sanity. Though, I'm sure none of you could understand that.

To me, it feels normal. But that's alright. I do not expect you to comprehend the conclusions that my brain tends to come to. Y'all are so boring. I suppose if I were to attempt to put my thoughts and actions into words, I'd express that it's all just an impulse behavior. I precisely do as I feel at the moment. Not really sure I see that as a problem, but apparently other people do. Ah, well. I believe they mentioned something about a low orbital cortex? Though I don't particularly listen, I could be wrong.

Anyhow, sometimes I have some really odd thoughts and dreams here. Like the other night I dreamt that *my* arm was literally decomposing. Like the flesh was falling off and there were maggots eating through what was left. Pretty horrific, yet ultimately it didn't really bother me. Why do I need my arm anymore? I've used it for everything I needed. Then, today, I saw a *jack-in-the-box start turning itself*. Weird shit. But

I like it. Oh, gotta go, the big guys are about to roll through here. Talk soon, probably.

Sometime Early January 1971

After I became used to my new routine in life, I was walking Gene down to the market. I actually decided to cook dinner that night since I had a decent kitchen. I felt so fancy in my new home. Moving had been a hassle. The first time I moved, I didn't have anything so it was pretty damn easy. But this time I had acquired a bunch of random shit, including a dog. Took me about a week to box up all my useless items, and another week to clean the place, but that part was just pure laziness cause of how much I hated cleaning. I found most of my boxes in a closet at my office, and the rest were leftovers given to me by the local market. I didn't see the need to take any of my own crappy furniture since Bettie's house was well furnished, so I dropped all my junk in the dumpster, loaded all my boxes in the bed of my truck, turned in my keys, and I was off.

It took me about 45 minutes of strolling up and down the aisles before I realized that I did not know how to cook anything halfway decent. So, I started walking over to the deli to pick up some sliced meat and some rolls, but ended up opting with canned chicken.

On my way to the checkout line, I ran into Fay. I can remember she was wearing a beautiful white dress with yellow sunflowers all over it. Wow! She looked stunning, and for the first time ever I was nervous to talk to her. Good thing she approached me first, otherwise I'm fairly sure I would have awkwardly pretended not to notice her. I hadn't seen her since Bettie passed, and I'm sure she had been wondering where I had gone because I wasn't living next to her anymore.

We had our usual small talk—she asked me where I had moved to, and then she asked what I was doing for the rest of the evening. I explained my embarrassing inability to cook, which then led to her insisting she come see my new home and prepare me a proper meal. I accepted. She had already purchased everything she planned on cooking so I put away my items and my empty basket, picked out some cheap white wine, and we were on our way. It was about a five-minute walk from the store and Fay had ridden her bike. It was yellow, just like the sunflowers on her dress, with a white basket attached to the handles, so I sped walk next to her as she pedaled beside me.

The night went surprisingly well for two people who had spent the last couple of years barely speaking to one another. She prepared for us some sort of fancy Hispanic dish. Who knows what it was called, but it was delicious, and not even close to the most important topic of the night... We talked a lot about her family and past. None about mine. *You can tell a lot about a person by listening to the way they talk about someone they once loved.*

But I did tell her the story of how I ended up in the Farghue house and how I missed Ms. Bettie. I think she felt bad for me because she reached over and hugged me; definitely not a feeling I was used to. We finished our bottle and called it a night. I offered my presence in the near future, but I'll talk more about that later. It would've been nice to have some permanent company around; but then again, I do enjoy being alone. I always have.

I took the next day off, cause I was my own boss and I had that ability to do what I wanted. I thought I would wander down to the pond where Bettie, ya know... I mean she was like a mother to me so I wanted to go visit her. All I was thinking was "I hope fish don't eat her body" but who was I kidding. That would be unfortunate. I wonder what she was thinking about whilst she took her last breath. Walter? Me? Nothing? I can only imagine she went into a state of panic, as she was being pulled deeper and deeper under.

I've heard somewhere that it's impossible to drown yourself with no constraints, so I am sure she tried to untie herself. I mean, it is a natural instinct to survive, even if you don't want to. Most people just shoot themselves and make it quick, but she chose to go down with some self-respect I guess. She didn't have the strength to untie herself though, because her lungs were reflexively filling up with water from silently screaming for help. Her body probably felt hot from losing so much oxygen and her brain more than likely felt like it was going to burst as everything around her went black. Then, eyes wide open, she stopped moving, knowing she was about to die. And that was it.

No one will ever get to see her again. What happens after everything goes black? That's the number one question. What happens when you're dead? If there's a God, dear God do I hope she ended up above the stars, rather than below the Earth. I hope she got what she wanted. Anyway, I sat on this medium-sized rock, about as big as a bench, that was located in the shallow end of the pond and I, essentially, talked out loud to her about my... date? I felt like Ms. Bettie would tell me something along the lines of, "Go for it Graham, go steady with the gal, it'll be good for you!" So maybe that's why I went to talk to her, because I knew she would tell me to do what I was already thinking about doing, and I needed that second shove. I know she didn't want me to end up like her, alone for the rest of my life just because I didn't want to fall in love again. So I was going to do whatever I had to do to give it a shot. *Take some chances.* Can't hurt anything.

After about an hour of Gene and I hanging out at the pond, we decided to walk over to the bar, ya know, to have a Scotch. It was time to get back to my daily Scotch ritual. It was one of those days where drinking at noon sounded like a decent idea.

Scotty let me bring Gene in; he always had some leftover scraps for him to chew on. I didn't really feel like telling him about my evening with Fay quite yet, so I just let him talk about his girl most of the time, with some random side conversation in between. I was trying to contemplate how I was going to ask Fay out. Do I go to her apartment? Do I wait to run into her again at the store? I don't want to be a creep but I didn't know how else to reach her. I decided I would find some sunflowers and leave them on her doorstep with a cute little note and a sucker attached to it. She wouldn't be able to resist.

Earlier that day on my way to the pond I passed by Meer Murphy Creek to open the gates. I thought it only fair that people should be allowed to mourn their family even though I wasn't fully ready to return to work yet. There was a younger male waiting by the gates when I opened them. He came in, laid a couple sunflowers down on one of the tombstones, and left... I thought he wouldn't mind if I borrowed them. And that I did. Right after the bar, I stopped by the graveyard, snatched the flowers off of Harriet Glurke's grave, and went to the office to prepare a note. I did own the damn place after all—what were they gonna do to me? Fire me? I felt bad for a few seconds or so, but I didn't give a damn after that. They were just gonna shrivel up and die anyway; I figured it'd be more useful to give them to someone who could actually smell and see them. I didn't know it at the time, but that was the start of it all...

Hello Fay,

I thoroughly enjoyed our evening together the other night and would much appreciate it if you would let me attempt to cook something for you? Or perhaps I could take you out somewhere? You made me feel something I've not felt in a really long time and I'd like to see if it goes somewhere. The world tends to fall in love with the best parts of people—happiness, looks, the way they laugh, etc. but I want to fall in love with the worst parts of you. You know that's the only kind of love that lasts and I hope you'll let me.

Patiently waiting, Graham Embry Soyle

I thought I had scared her off, seeing as though a week had passed and I hadn't seen or heard from her. But, worry not, because one day on my way to work I passed her on the sidewalk and she explained that she had forgotten where I lived, therefore she could not get into contact with me. A huge weight was lifted. I actually involuntarily smiled for once. Come to think of it now, she knew where I worked. If she really wanted to get in touch with me she could have stopped by the graveyard. Anyways, she said she loved the sunflowers. She said my words were "sweet." "Why does she like me?" I thought. Well I suppose asking her wasn't really an option, so I would just go along with it to see if it lasted. And it did. We stayed strong for a while. She would bring me lunch at the graveyard, and in return, I would visit her for a night-time smoke after my shift. We small talked for awhile. It took me a few months to start trusting her enough to let her in on my thoughts and my past. Even then, I never really told her about my father. Kind of told her stuff without telling her any of the bad stuff. I didn't want to seem too damaged. But then again, it would be nice to let someone in. There was so much I needed to let off my chest then, even now sometimes. Could she have been the one?

You'll just have to wait because it's time for my afternoon job now. Time surprisingly went by fast today.

Graham Embry Soyle
10/03/06

93

POINSETTIAS

GOOD CHEER AND SUCCESS

DECEMBER, 1971

A *great time for me.* A few months had passed since I had taken over the graveyard and said goodbye to Bettie. Fay and I had been dating for almost a full year at that point, and it was finally Christmas time. I hadn't celebrated Christmas since I was younger. So, it was nice to have someone who wanted to decorate and celebrate a holiday together. It wasn't the same as it was back in Kansas. In Meerdin, people actually came together and did stuff. It was... different. I liked it. People seemed so happy there.

But most importantly, Fay seemed happy and that's all that mattered, as long as I contributed to putting a smile on her face, that's all I cared about. For a while anyway. For a while I felt kind of normal, though that did not last long. I could only act as if I cared for human interaction for so long. I wasn't very good at pretending; still not. Do I really need to care for people? I know I can't be the only one here who has no feelings. Well, I have feelings... I know they are there. But it's as if two people are standing across a great chasm: I stand there and across the way I see another me who is tortured and beaten every day by what he should be feeling. And though I know it's sad, there is nothing I can do for him. There is *no* way for me to get to him. But every now and then, when the chasm is filled with alcohol, I am able to swim across and shoulder the burden. But when I wake I am always back on the other side. Regardless, Christmas '70 was a good time, it was a good year. I am glad we had the chance to spend it together.

Christmas used to be my Mama's favorite holiday. She was always her happiest when it was that time of year. She would start counting down the days no later than when labor day hit, and certainly never waiting 'til Thanksgiving to put up the tree. It's not like she was given any expensive presents or anything. I mean, we didn't even sit down for dinner or roast marshmallows by the fire. It was just another day for my father to work and sleep.

To tell you the truth, I'm not sure why Mama loved Christmas so much, but I always looked forward to seeing her smile during that month every year. Christmas Day, Mama would dress up in a velvet green peacoat and trudge through the snow to go to church for the 8 AM service. My father would never go because he didn't like getting dressed up. He never really believed anyways, not like my Mama did. I used to go with her in my younger years so I remember how different she was when she was at church. She lit up with joy, and smiled as she sang along with the harmonizing choir, always with her eyes closed, as if she was dreaming the whole time. She would look up towards the sky and say a prayer and a happy birthday to God. After the early morning service, she would take a warm cup of cocoa and a chocolate chip cookie from the table and head out the doors.

The years I would go with her, we would go around to the side of the church and lay down in the snow, spreading our legs and arms out as far as they could reach so we could make our own little angels. See, I used to believe in God when I was young because I would just follow what my Mama believed in. I wanted to be like her so I did as she did. She had faith, there-fore so did I. That all changed though when I saw who He really created and put on this earth. My father started shoving bottles down his throat in my early teenage years, around 12 or 13 I'd say. He became so angry after drinking, and he never put down the whiskey, so he was always angry. He would lash out at my Mama for no reason at all, hit her across the face, kick her in the back, throw her against the wall... you name it, he did it all.

One day, he struck her so hard against the face, drops of blood started to fall from her head, right at her hairline. After that day, I lost what little faith I had and I never went back to the church with Mama again. It was too hard for me to cope with the appraisal of one man after having seen such terrible things in my life already. If God's duty was to protect the peo-ple of the earth, then why place bad people here with the good ones? How could He allow my father to beat my Mama over the head, especially after Mama paid so much respect towards Him? It's not that I don't believe in Him anymore—it's that

He hasn't shown to me why I should have faith. Nothing good has ever happened to me, nothing good has ever happened to anybody I ever knew. I watched my Mama be faithful to Him for so many years, and now look where she is. In "heaven?" Yeh right. She is decomposing somewhere, whether it's six feet underneath the ground, or still on that cold laminate flooring.

She's not walking through some golden gates in the sky, sleeping on a pillow of clouds, and watching over me right now. It's not that I don't believe in *something*, I mean I'd love for there to be something after I leave this life. Do I think it has anything to do with Jesus Christ? No. Transforming into an inanimate object? Definitely not. Am I going to be worm food? More than likely, yes. But, I am open to whatever comes after death. I have always been ready for new ideas and I'll keep that state of mind until I'm gone.

Yeh, my Mama became upset with me when I lost my faith, but she always maintained her blissful mindset on Christmas day. She still kept her same routine, even after the drinking started, and maintained her faith until her life was taken away from her.

Tuesday, December 14th, 1971

Was a sad day for Scotty. We had planned to take our ladies to the holiday parade in Philadelphia that night. I had only traveled to Philly one time before that and I liked it pretty well. Got to see the Liberty Bell, which was kinda anticlimactic if you ask me. Also the Edgar House; it was very informative, a lot larger than I ever imagined. Always nice to get to know about the life of someone you've never met. Oh and my favorite part was this little Irish Pub called McGillin's—oldest bar in Philly, or maybe all of the U.S. I can't remember.

Anyway, it was really cool. Apparently the back door that leads to an alleyway was the same alley that the prohibitionists used to escape from and they would come into that bar to get away. They had kept mostly everything exactly the way it was when it was built in 1860, and they have never closed since then. The food was pretty great, too, so I definitely planned on taking them all there. Before we left I stopped by Lloyd's Locals to grab a pack of Dovals, two six packs of Little Kings, and a few spicy jerky sticks for the road. I started up my truck for the first time in four years.

I mean, I had to drive it from Clover Apartments to Bettie's when I moved, but other than that I hadn't driven a distance in my truck since my solo road trip to nowhere. I was scared of the truck not being able to run properly, but it seemed to be functioning just fine. I picked Scotty and Christina up from the bar, got Fay from her apartment complex, and we were on the way to Pennsylvania. As we drove through the highway traffic for two hours we switched from driver to passenger to the bed of the truck. It was only a two-door so we had to take turns as to who got to sit inside.

We all discussed how content we were with our lives at that point in time. We discussed and laughed about our futures together and how we would be driving to the parade when we were old and wrinkled, even though I think we all knew that wouldn't be happening. We drank both six-packs on the way to the city and I remember smoking half a pack of cigarettes on the way, too. I was having fun for the first time in a long time. Christina became quiet on the second half of the drive, and she wasn't drinking anything or smoking at all that night, which I thought was strange. When we arrived, we didn't know what to expect because it was our first and only time ever attending Nuremberg Christkind at the Philadelphia Christmas Market. It was a huge market that was modeled after the events in Germany.

There were dark pitchers of beer everywhere, salted pretzels, and bread with chocolate dip. People were dressed in strange, authentic outfits that looked very thick and warming. I believe they were called "Lederhosen." Loud music to dance to, stands to shop at, and a wonderful parade to watch. I really enjoyed going to that market, and we probably would have gone back every single year if it wasn't for what happened around 7 PM that night. Scotty and I went off in search of some flowers from one of the market stands for our girls. This beautiful shade of red caught my eye. It was as bright as a fire truck, bright as splattered blood as soon as it hits oxygen. The poinsettia truly is a beautiful flower, meant for a beautiful woman. I went and delivered my flourishing red beauty to Fay and she absolutely loved it.

We watched Scotty give his to Christina from afar, and she started bawling as soon as she saw it. It looked like they were in the middle of an argument... she pushed him aside and ran in the opposite direction. I later found out that the poinsettia brought up some memories of Christina's past Christmases back home. She ultimately decided to return to Minnesota to be with family and chose that path instead of a future life she could've had with Scotty. To my surprise, Fay bolted off that night to join and comfort her, even though they weren't particularly close or anything. Scotty and I were left standing alone in a mass of drunk Germans.

When it was time to leave around midnight, Fay returned to us to relay the bad news. Christina wouldn't be coming back to Meerdin that night with us. She said she was catching a ride back in a day or so. The ride back to Delaware that night was completely silent. Scotty never saw Christina after that winter evening. We did find out that when she returned to Meerdin, it was just to pack up her belongings and move back home to Minnesota. Too bad. I really liked her for Scott.

Graham Embry Soyle
10/06/06

CHRYSANTHEMUMS

The sun and the light

Sunday, February 12th, 1972

Fay and I had just reached our year mark a few weeks before, and I was looking forward to taking the next step with her on Valentine's Day that year. I was going to ask her to move in with me and say goodbye to the Clover Apartment complex forever. She had been spending more and more time with me at the Farghue house anyway, so it seemed fitting that she had a permanent spot at my place. Fay met me at Murphy Creek around noon that day, like she usually did. But this time she didn't bring me lunch, she didn't bring me anything actually, which was very unusual considering the routine we had accommodated. I was raking leaves in the yard when I saw her walking over to me. I smiled at her, and she didn't smile back. Her face was blushed as if she had just finished crying. She came up to me and I quickly leaned in to peck her on the lips, but she snapped her neck to the right, making sure her lips didn't come into contact with mine.

"What did I do?" I thought to myself. Then she poured it all out... "Graham, I love you. I really do love you. I just don't love you enough to keep myself here. I can't stay here forever just waiting for my life to begin. I want to go to school, I want to get a *real* job in the Big Apple, maybe on Wall Street. There's nothing in Meerdin for me anymore, not even your smile is enough to keep me going. Come with me, and we can be together," she explained to me. What was I going to do in the city? Nothing. I couldn't leave the graveyard and let Bettie down. I wasn't ready for that. So, I declined her offer to move to the city with her, and watched her turn around and walk out the gate. She said nothing else. That was my only chance, and I threw it away.

Where did this all come from? Why had I never heard about her wanting to move to the city and go to school? Why did it take her a year to figure that out and just bring it up out of nowhere? I just didn't understand. But at least Fay was being honest with me about her thoughts, when I was truly never honest with her about mine. I never expressed to her how messed up my life really was and what demented thoughts ran through my brain at every second throughout the day.

She wouldn't have wanted to be with me anyhow so it's a good thing I never truly opened up to her. I didn't feel hatred towards her because I knew that she would have a much better life without me. I always felt I was holding her back when we were together. The only thing I really felt was disappointment. But luckily that wasn't the last time I saw her. I turned around to get back to work and a blotch of warm colors caught my eye. Near the base of a headstone, a small bouquet lay wilting in the midday sun. I walked over to take a second and admire the scene, thinking back to my flower book.

Chrysanthemums, a flower that comes in almost any color, and has twice as many meanings. The ones at my feet represent love, trust, and a new life. Given my particular occupation at the time, I learned it's inherent variety also makes it one of the most popular flowers of choice for a funeral. A sad smile parted my lips... how ironic.

That same day after work I decided to go meet Scotty at the bar to have a shot. It had only been a couple of months since Christina broke up with him, and I still never knew exactly why they didn't work out, so I thought I would talk about my feelings with him and see how long it took him to get over Christina. After three shots of Scotch, and half of a glass of a Whiskey-Coke, Scotty was telling me everything I wanted to know.

It turns out that Scotty's girl had a conversation with him that was similar to the one Fay had with me. It seemed that the both of us were holding our women back in life. I guess I was a loser. I *still am* a loser. Scotty and I needed to let loose that night, forget about the women that didn't want us, and find tall, beautiful, cheerful, blondes that did want us. So, shot by shot we took. We decided to move to another bar called "The Shooter." It was just a couple of blocks down the road from our bar, and by the time we walked there, the eight shots of Scotch had reached our brains. I was not thinking straight at all. It felt like my brain was in another body and I could barely walk straight. Scott didn't look to be faring much better. It was by far the most drunk I had ever been, but I wasn't worried about the painstakingly brutal hangover that was going to follow the next morning; I was just focused on forgetting the past and having a good, drunken night. Forget the barbaric scene of my Mama spread out on the kitchen flooring with buckets of blood surrounding her. Forget the gruesome letter left by Bettie that was shockingly too detailed. Block out the twisted thoughts that ran through my mind on a daily basis. Forget it all!

And so I did, for a little while at least. She was absolutely gorgeous. She was sitting at a table in the corner of the bar, sipping on a vodka-Shirley Temple. She was bubbly, blonde, and busty. Screwing a dumb blonde was all I needed to make the pain of Fay go away. Something about my mysterious attitude made her interested enough in me to come back to my house that night, and I was ecstatic. I don't remember much about the bar scene or anything that was said to her or the journey to my house due to how drunk I was, but I do remember screwing her brains out. I was so focused on it. I knew that chances were, I would never see that woman again, so I wanted to make it worth her while. If only she had known how insane my mind worked... perhaps she would've chosen to turn me down that night... She was sporting a sexy red brassiere with matching panties, and her porcelain skin was glistening even in the darkness of my bedroom.

I threw her down on the checkered-patterned comforter and traced her hip bones with my fingers, traveling up to her chest where I clumsily removed her bra, unhooking it in the back and ripping it off from the front with my teeth. Then, of course, I gently slithered my hands down her back until I was down far enough to remove her underwear, attempting to barely touch my fingertips to her skin while doing it so she would get that ticklish feeling. Her curves were something else. I couldn't stop myself from tracing her entire body up and down with my hands, as if I was sculpting her myself.

She was giggling the entire time, probably because she was so intoxicated, but that sting of alcohol in my nervous system made the sensual feelings intensify to levels I can't even explain. As astonishing as it was, I had never had drunk sex before, but its power allows me to remember it still, to this day. The veins in my penis were throbbing, they were pounding to the exact beat of my heart. I remember her laying there like a ragdoll, too out of her mind to even fathom how hard she was about to get fucked. She may have even been unconscious, come to think of it, but she wanted it. I *knew* she wanted it. Holding the base of the shaft, I guided myself into her tight, drowning, hole and forcefully shoved the tip all the way until I couldn't go any further.

Meanwhile I struck my mouth to her neck and sucked so hard that it alone would have made her orgasm. It was a completely new sensation that I had never before felt. Every bone in my body was trembling, I was sweating profusely, and my dick was throbbing so intensely, it felt as if it grew two sizes with each pulse. I pounded and pounded her into the headboard, attempting to make her cum even though she was probably too drunk to notice anyway. She wasn't screaming with joy but I bet she had an immensely terrific dream because she couldn't stop dragging her long nails up and down my back. Faster and faster I slammed her into the wall, grabbing her neck and squeezing it as I went. I could tell she enjoyed it by the way she was grabbing my forearms.

I never knew I enjoyed rough sex until that night. I took my dick out for a second and went down on her just to stir my anxiety up a little bit. I don't know how to describe it, but when I get so close to an orgasm, and then just completely cut it off, I want it so much more than I wanted it a few seconds earlier. It felt like a million little men were running around poking inside the skin of my shaft with their tiny little dwarf fingers. It felt as if they were trying to escape but I wouldn't let them just yet.

I fought the urge to erupt until the anticipation passed, and then, lifting her leg up above my shoulder, I jammed myself back inside of her again. Along with a gallon of cum, came 25 years of trauma, all of my demented thoughts and fears, and any adrenaline I had left in me. I immediately passed out on top of her. If she died in the middle of the night, at least I'm for certain she experienced that powerful moment.

She woke up that next morning underneath me, not sure of what had happened that previous evening. She didn't even know my name, yet she still managed to rise from bed and prepare us some oatmeal and apple juice. I decided to break the awkwardness that was in the room and ask for her name. I mean, who knew? Perhaps we could have taken off... gone steady for a while. I wanted to try my best with her because, even though I didn't really know who she was, we had a great night.

"Daisy Dahlman," she said. I smirked and replied, "Graham Embry Soyle." A feeling came over me like when I hurt my cow, Betsy. I never saw her again after that morning. Actually, nobody did. There was an ad in the paper the next week with the headline "MISSING." If I remember correctly, she was never found. Too bad... She was very essential to my great night of pleasure.

Graham Embry Soyle
10/10/06

VIOLET

MODESTY

MONDAY, APRIL 10TH, 1972

The day I realized that my life was a ticking-time bomb. Everyone I came into contact with either died, left, went missing, moved, killed themselves, or became uninterested. I couldn't keep anybody in my life, so I decided to just stop trying. I needed to focus on myself at that time in my life. I wanted to do something other than just dig graves and open and lock the gate everyday. I was passionate about *something*, I just wasn't sure what it was yet. Let me think back. I was fond of smoking, drinking, walking Gene, sleeping, talking with Scott and Ingrid occasionally, going to Sal's, and... reading my flower book. That's the one thing outside of basic human life that I was fascinated with. I truly admired each petal I saw, ya know each one felt and smelled differently. I could never get enough of it... I made a game out of it actually. I would read my flower book, and pick out a particular type that interested me. I would have to find that specific flower in the yard somewhere on one of the tombstones, and I would tear off one petal from the plant and glue it to the page in the book with the corresponding species.

The game was over when every page had a petal glued to it. Never did finish that damn game... just like everything else I ever did in my life... people are just too original. "If you love a flower, don't pick it up. Because if you pick it up it dies and it ceases to be what you love. So if you love a flower, let it be. Love is not about possession. Love is about appreciation. — Osho" was written on page 48 of *The Golden Guide* and it has stuck with me ever since I saw it.

I wish I had realized how true that quote was earlier on in life. Ya know, like May of '69 would have been a good time to figure it out. When I saw that small, weak, dirty ball of fur, and I fell in love, all I wanted was for him to be my own. I wanted him and that's all I cared about. I didn't appreciate his beauty, or his life for what it was. I picked him up, took him home, and made him adjust to a new life with me. I should have just let him be. But no, I completely went against every aspect of this quote and destroyed a beautiful flower.

If I would have kept on biking and left Gene limp off by himself down the road, then we wouldn't have become so close over the years. We wouldn't have been best friends, and we never would've experienced so many amazing memories together, which in turn would have made his passing a hell of a lot easier.

But... life's not easy, obviously.

The most common symptoms of a brainstem tumor are instability and weakness on one side of the body. Tilting of the head, a staggered walk, difficulty with swallowing, loss of appetite, and vomiting. Or at least that's what they told me after it was too late to matter. I also noticed a change in Gene's bark, loss in the mobility of his eyes, and slight paralysis on his right side. Unfortunately, he had to suffer through all of these symptoms for a while, considering his owner was a dumbass who couldn't perceive his suffering. I think that on May 3rd, 1969, Gene was starting to feel the agony of his tumor, which would explain the sweet whimpering coming from his little body that spring morning when I found him. Sometimes, it's too difficult to think about the loss of him. Sometimes I can't get through it, but I'm going to try for you right now. If there was one thing I did right in my life, it was love Gene, and I deserve credit for at least that. I want you to know how painful it was to say goodbye.

FRIDAY, JULY 21ST, 1972

Gene and I went for an evening walk around town, just like the normal routine. He always walked right beside me or behind me at all times, so I never really noticed him. He was always someone to talk to, and I felt no reason to look at him. It's not like I could look him in the eye or anything due to my being five feet taller than him.

Anyways, this evening, my right bootlace tripped me as I was walking and knocked my cigarette out of my hand, right into a puddle on the ground. I knelt down, angered by my clumsiness, and began to tie my wet laces back into a knot. Most of the time I would just tuck them in the sides of my shoe, but today I was feeling a bit more fancy. As I was tying my shoe, I glanced over at my knee and saw that I was wearing the same jeans from that one morning when I fell off my bike and ripped the denim right through to the bone. The same jeans that gave my puppy his precious name.

I looked up from my knee, and saw my handsome white ball of fur, my one true friend, walking along. That was the moment I realized he wasn't as bright-eyed and bushy-tailed as when I first picked him up that day. He actually looked terrible. He dragged himself along the pavement, not even noticing that I had stopped to tie my shoelaces. He could only move his front and back left paws, so he dragged his whole right side along, which led to the fur on that side being stained with mud and dirt and to be matted down close to his skin. His tail had no hair on it anymore, only a few patches remained, which made it look even worse.

Gene could barely see anymore, and he kept running into bushes and fences along the sidewalk. At one point during that evenings' walk, he stopped walking altogether. I think he finally realized he was walking alone, but he just rested there, panting for a moment or two. I'll never forget the look on his precious face when he glanced back at me and nodded. It was almost like he was telling me "everything is going to be okay" like when my mother would tell me that. It brought me joy and sadness at the same time, but more sadness because he looked at me dead in the face with his glossy eyes. Since I was kneeling, we were finally eye-level and I got the chance to really look at him and examine every detail about his face. His eyes were barely open, his nose was wet, and I could see him shivering. Through all that, I still managed to see him as the whimpering baby from two years before that. I thought of all the amazing memories we had shared together over this time. I knew my time with Gene had to come to an end. I just wasn't ready for it to happen yet. And it didn't... for a short while at least.

My fascination with flowers made me think one day, "Why do we not have a flower shop in Meerdin?" I knew the answer already. It was because Mr. Brady's shop in Dover was good enough for everybody in town. Mr. Brady grew the flowers himself, I believe, and sold them in his shop in bouquets, arrangements, singles, dozens...there were always tulips, baby's breath, carnations, lilies, chrysanthemums, violets, and other common kinds. I only knew this cause Bettie mentioned it to me one time that that was the place she recommended to the cemetery visitors.

I also knew that if I opened my own shop in Meerdin, business would be booming. People that brought flowers to their loved ones at Murphy Creek despised travelling into the city to buy them, I was sure of it. "How easy would it be if someone could walk to my flower shop, and then walk right down the road to deliver them?" I thought. I knew I had to go through with it. I just didn't know how I would supply the beautiful plants. I'm not sure that I am responsible enough to keep up with my own garden, keeping something alive? Ha. Though I surprisingly had enough money to fund a small business like that, thanks to Bettie's third key. Took a week or two before I came to the realization that the answer was directly in front of me the entire time. The cemetery. It was right there.

Every day people just handed their flowers over to me. It was as if I had created a giant donation center, where they were bringing them just so that I could start a new business. Yes!

Well, that's what I told myself in order to justify it. Sure, I may have been a horrible person, stealing flowers from those grieving humans, but, in my defense, they did it to themselves. It was either me who took them and put them to good use, or the little possums that would eventually get to them and eat them during the night. I think my use for them was the better of the two options. For now, I want to tell you about the night that I officially stole from the graveyard. Not those damn sunflowers I borrowed a while back for Fay... that shit was childish and unexpected. This was the real deal.

MONDAY, APRIL 30TH, 1973

Was such a rush, the feeling of accomplishment I got, sneaking around the cemetery, searching for the perfect, still intact flowers. Creeping in the dark, Gene beside me as my partner in crime, until I snatched the ones I wanted. Running out the gate exit, sprinting until my low lung tolerance couldn't take it any longer. Running until I fell and hit the ground, landing on top of those *dead, crushed* violet flowers I had just stolen.

Even though I ruined them, it was such a rush knowing I got away with it. No one was there to see me, that I knew of. I mean, how could they be? I was the only one with the key. And it just felt so good. Could I seriously have been the first person to think of this idea? I knew it was going to work. I knew this is what I was going to start doing. It's what I never knew I always wanted to do.

My passion for flowers was about to become so much more. I already had the idea where I was going to set up shop if it was still available. The vacant building next to the bar that had been for *sale* for god knows how long. It would be mine, I just had to pick out a name for it. Something significant. Something that would stand out. Something that would bring people in. I'm not really sure why I wasted so much time thinking about what I would name the shop when I already knew deep down I would end up naming it after my beloved Mama.

So that is exactly what I did. Lynn's Petals. It was something I could call my own, something that I had a connection with. I loved it. I thought it was going to be a lot more work, seeing as I was buying a building and all, but it wasn't. It wasn't even the original owner that met up with me when I called the faded number on the sign. It was his gorgeous daughter that I'm sure I could've courted for a while, but I chose to not approach her in fear of losing my cherished place. I signed some papers, handed over a money order that I got from my bank earlier that morning and that was it.

Granted, there was a lot to do with the place. Ceiling needed some work, there wasn't a working bathroom, the walls... oh my god, the walls. Needless to say, this place hadn't had a single foot touch the floor in years. I'm surprised that a homeless person wasn't shacked up inside. But all that was okay with me. I got a good deal, Carl finally sold his space, and everyone was happy. It was all very exciting. I thought it'd be pretty fun to do it all up exactly how I wanted. Ya know it would keep me busy, not like I had anything (or anyone) else to do anyway. It helped that I hired some random young kid I met at Lloyd's one morning. His name was Blake. He mentioned he wanted some extra money to save for a car and I figured it wouldn't hurt to have an extra set of hands and some company. He lasted a little bit... probably not as long as he expected, but ya know... shit happens. He ended up being in the wrong place at the wrong time. I'll tell you about that later...

Colors were the most difficult thing for me to decide upon. So many options... couldn't be too bright, or too dull. It couldn't be my favorite color cause I didn't want to let anyone know anything about me. It couldn't be my Mama's favorite color cause I had already named the place after her. Couldn't paint it white because that's too common. Surely I didn't want to put up any of that god-awful wallpaper that seemed to cover the walls of every house, restaurant, and store in town.

So finally, after days and days of contemplating my thoughts out loud to Gene, we decided to go with violet. I chose violet because it was the first flower that made me feel alive. It was the first flower that made me feel like I had a purpose. It wasn't too bright, yet not too dark. It had a nice calming effect. It was perfect.

Graham Embry Soyle
10/12/06

PAPAVER RHOEAS

SLEEP, PEACE, AND DEATH

TUESDAY, MAY 1ST, 1973

fter my eight hours at Meer Murphy Creek, I went to
Meerdin's local hardware store and picked out the perfect
violet paint. Oh, and obviously brushes, buckets, and
other miscellaneous painting shit. I also picked up a couple
things necessary to fix up the place, ya know the basic wall
decorations, floor mats, tables, lamps, shelves, etc. I bought
an assortment of vases and fertilizer packets and decided to
wait on any other supplies until I was almost ready to open. I
ran into Ingrid while I was there.

She went on and on about how I looked like such a handy-
man and how her back porch light had stopped working... ya
know, she wanted me to come over and "look at it for her." I
knew what *that* meant, but I just took the compliment and

went on with my day. She was a little too desperate sometimes. Makes you wonder what happened to her in her past to make her act so coquettish all the time.

Besides, I hadn't even turned on the electricity in my own new store yet; certainly wasn't going to go fix someone else's problems before my own. So, I painted with whatever sunlight creeped through the doors and windows that day. It was almost too perfect because the back window overlooked a huge grassy field that was almost completely covered in papaver rhoeas flowers.

I told you about Bettie's husband being in the military, right?

Well, after looking up the details of this flower, which most commonly is called the Red Poppy, I found out that it symbolizes fallen soldiers. It's not even a U.S. native flower, which means someone took a specific effort to plant these flowers here.

Can't believe in all the years that I've been here, I've never even noticed them. It was almost a sign.

I mean it was her money that gave me the opportunity to buy this place to begin with and since her tragic passing, I have never felt closer to her.

That phrase caught my attention though; *fallen soldiers*. Why was this flower affiliated with this?

So I looked more into it. The more I searched and searched, I wound up discovering that this soldier, John McCrae, wrote a poem about his best friend who was killed by a German shell and as he sat in the back of the ambulance the next day he wrote a poem and handed it to Allison, the sergeant delivering mail:

"*His face was very tired but calm as he wrote. He looked around from time to time, his eyes straying to Helmer's grave,*" she said. The poem read—

In Flanders fields the poppies blow
Between the crosses, row on row,
That mark our place: and in the sky
The larks still bravely singing fly
Scarce heard amid the guns below.
We are the dead: Short days ago,
We lived, felt dawn, saw sunset glow,
Loved and were loved: and now we lie
In Flanders fields!
Take up our quarrel with the foe
To you, from failing hands, we throw
The torch: be yours to hold it high
If ye break faith with us who die,
We shall not sleep, though poppies grow
In Flanders fields

*(Composed at the battlefront on May 3, 1915
during the second battle of Ypres, Belgium, John McCrae)*

121

Anyways, that was why, that day, the papaver rhoeas would forever be symbolized as red poppies blowing in the wind amongst the many crosses that mark the resting places of fallen soldiers. I only remember it because I memorized it so that I could use it as a pickup line. Poets are really appealing to women, believe it or not.

I memorized the entirety of that poem the first couple times I read it, and to this day I've never forgotten it. Hope that I never do. It's something that people should know. It's something that *should* be remembered. And that's why I'm sharing it with you now. I hope that you won't forget it either.

Saturday, June 8th, 1974

It was probably around 8 or 9 PM when I got this kind of weird feeling that I needed a Scotch, so I went to see Scotty.

I looked up at the TV they had recently bought and sat at the very end of the bar.

Little House on the Prairie was playing. I hated that show, so I asked if he could change the station. He flipped through the channels a couple times and landed on the news. A huge tornado had hit Topeka a couple hours prior.

Apparently it was rated an F4, which is apparently the second worst kind of tornado. It took out a lot of people. Looked pretty bad... It was the same date as the one that hit back in 1966.

Man I'll never forget that one. Glad I finally left that death trap.

Well, sorry for that pointless memory. On to the next!

Thursday, August 29th, 1974

I woke up later than usual. Gene was always my alarm clock but he didn't come into my room and bark that morning. I glanced up at the clock hanging on the wall and saw that it was around 10:30 AM, which means there was no point in going to work that day, considering I was already late. I rolled out of the bed, and found myself stepping in a pile of vomit on my way to the bathroom. I cleaned my feet off, took an exhilarating piss, and brushed my teeth half assedly over the sink.

I walked out into the living room and hollered for Gene, but he didn't come around the corner wagging his tail. I had no idea where he was, but I decided to make some breakfast. Maybe the smell of bacon would have him running towards me. Two eggs, two servings of potatoes, four bacon strips, and two slices of toast later, I found myself eating alone at the table. It was noon now, and I was starting to get irritated.

I felt like he was my toddler child that was messing with me and playing hide n' seek and just waiting in a closet somewhere to be found. It was fun for a second, and then it became too much. I needed to find him, I needed to find Gene so we could spend a day off together and take a walk, and make him listen to my pointless daily rants.

I checked outside, under my bed, and around all of the sinks. I spent a while running around the house like a madman, when really I had an idea of where he was the entire time. I just didn't want to bring myself to check his favorite spot in the house, right behind the flower-printed sofa, in the corner up against the wall. I popped my head through the space between the back of the couch and the wall and I started to cry because I saw a glimpse of white at the far end of the space. "G-Gene," I whimpered. No movement. I pushed the sofa out with one giant shove, and there he was, laying there, motionless, lifeless. I pretended he was sleeping peacefully, and I watched him for a moment.

I was waiting for him to quiver a little bit or roll over and stretch, but nothing ever happened. I scooped him up in my arms and petted him on his beautiful white fur. He still felt warm but stiff. He still felt full of life, yet not at all. Something fell from his mouth when I pulled him up close to my chest and I reached to grab it. It was his tiny jean collar I had made him when I first got him. I thought I had lost it months before that, but I guess he still had it all along, hidden in his spot. I was so lucky to have had Gene as a dog for the time that I did. He helped me adjust to a new town, break away from some sadness in my life. He was my first friend. He was with me while I was mourning for Bettie, and through my breakup with Fay. He was even with me when I started my flower business, and he'll forever be in my heart.

I can still remember when I took him to the vet to get flea medication and Dr. Lamina told me I should enjoy the next month with Gene because he didn't see him living past that point. I made myself forget about it because I didn't want to deal with it, but there we were 11 months past the predicted death from the veterinarian. Gene was a fighter. Stop it, Graham! Crying is a sign of weakness in here and it could get me killed so I have to go and dry my sorrow face and pretend as if I have no feelings.

Well, I've collected myself now, and I can't just leave it at that. Gene's life was worth more than that. After coming to terms with the loss of my best friend, it was obvious to me that I wasn't going to handle it well. I threw on those same ripped jeans from when I found Gene, a violet-colored pullover that I had found in Bettie's chests, and I bolted out the front door and down the street. I didn't want my bike, I didn't want my Little Kings, I didn't even want a cigarette... all I wanted was to run. I wanted to run far away and forget. Forget ever meeting that damn dog, forget ever taking him as my own, forget losing him too soon. I sprinted that night as far as my body allowed and I must've made four complete circles around town because I passed the graveyard four times that night. Somehow I ended up at the Lake of Wishes, ya know, Bettie's first resting place. I laid down in the dirt the entire night, from dusk to dawn, just thinking. I didn't close my eyes longer than the times I was forced to blink.

Sometimes I think about that. Blinking. It's one thing in life that we can't control. I mean, think about it. Try not to wink... for a minute? Maybe. For two minutes? You're an alien. For three minutes? Impossible. It just happens; your body forces itself to blink. I don't like the feeling—I feel like someone is controlling me. Breathing, too! Something else a person can't control.

Anyways, I lay there until the sun started to come up and then I decided it was time to test the theory. The theory about the Lake of Wishes was if a person was submerged in the lake at the break of dawn, one wish would be granted to them, no matter the absurdity of the wish. That was my one chance to be happy again, to truly have one thing that I wanted. I ripped off those jeans and pullover, stripped down to my bare skin, hoping that nobody was watching, and I dived into that lake.

I don't know what had gotten into me. I was never usually the one up for spontaneous morning swims in lakes where dead people lay, but something came over me that morning. Hope, I suppose. I dunked myself underwater and held my breath for as long as I possibly could. Do you want to know my wish? I wished that Gene was alive and well and that he wasn't sick anymore. I wished that over and over again about 30 or 40 times in my head until I ran out of air and shot out of the water, freezing my ass off.

I'll spare you the rest of this sob story and tell you that the Lake of Wishes is complete and utter bullshit. My dog didn't come back to life. He still lay limp right where I left him on the couch, wrapped in a blanket, snuggling his jean collar. I was so idiotic to even believe it would work.

I ran all the way home and burst through the front door with a smile on my face ready to welcome Gene back to reality, only to be kicked in the balls by my dignity. There are no granted wishes in life, no genies in lamps, no second chances. What's done is done, and there is no going back. I remember covering Gene up with that throw blanket, and running to my bed to cry.

Oh, and you want to know the best part about the whole damn thing? It's that I stepped in his vomit from earlier that morning right before jumping into bed.

It was warm and mushy, as if it was fresh from the stomach only seconds before. It smelled like roses that had been dead for three years mixed with the shit of a skunk, and I could feel the chunks in between my toes, as if they were sitting there mocking me. I guess I forgot to clean it up that morning. Sweet dreams, am I right?

Friday, August 30th, 1974

I placed Gene in a woven basket and covered him with a soft, baby blue blanket. I took him with me to work that day because I planned on burying him and having a little ceremony for him to say goodbye. Vern didn't know yet that Gene had passed, and obviously he couldn't see him when I carried him in, but it was as if he knew that something bad happened. He asked me where Gene was, and I just started crying. Vern, also crying at that point, took the basket from me and sat down in the grass with Gene's limp body. He was just holding him in his arms, rubbing his stomach, waiting for him to come back to life. I decided Vern needed closure almost more than I did, so together we dug a hole on the side of his house and placed Gene inside, basket and all, into the hole. We covered him back up with dirt, and with each shovel, we said something that we loved about Gene. I teared up when Vern started to hum "Crazy He Calls Me." He hummed the entire song almost twice before we finished. I guess Vern loves that song almost as much as my mother did.

Graham Embry Soyle
10/15/06

Tuesday, February 14th, 1961

My very first Valentine's Day that actually meant something

to me. My very first love, a day I'll never allow myself to forget. Do you remember being young? When nothing mattered in the world except your middle school crush and what you were going to be eating for dinner? Not a worry in the world.

Damn, I miss those days terribly. Though, I suppose now-a-days I don't have too much to worry about either. But that's besides the point. I miss being a teenager, even though my home life kinda sucked, I miss the times when I only had two things on my mind, not a million.

But seeing as though I'll never be able to go back in time physically, the best I can do is talk about it; that'll just have to do. So, anyways my first V-Day! I started the morning off by bringing my lovely lady some flowers, ya know back then I wasn't too obsessed with them, so I can't quite remember what kind I picked up from Bo-Nansas, but I got a 30-percent discount for working there, which was a lot to a 15-year-old. That alone would have kept a smile on her face for the rest of the day, but I wanted more: I wanted her heart to smile, I wanted her to re-fall in love that day.

I didn't want to be just another kid who was drooling over her meer perfection, I wanted to win her over, and by golly that's exactly what I did. Following my couple dozen of flowers, I handed her a box filled with Jolly Ranchers. I know, you expected to hear chocolate, but she didn't like chocolate, which made me love her even more. She didn't like the grape ones either, which made it harder for me cause I had to fish all the purple ones out and get rid of them.

She wasn't like anyone else I had ever met, and I didn't just think that because I was a horny teenager. I thought that because I was different, too, and I could see it. I knew I would never find someone as special as her, and to this day, I never have. When lunchtime came around, I convinced her to skip class with me and I took her to our favorite field for a perfect picnic of chips and PB&J sandwiches (also her favorite, of course). We laid there, hand in hand, as if nothing and no one else existed. I wish it didn't. I wish I had never left that moment. I wish I was still in Kansas, looking her in the eyes. I wish I had died that day, cause I would have died the happiest person in the world.

But I didn't. And I'm not. Anyway, after our long lunch, school was over by then so we rode our bikes back through the neighborhood racing—just wasting time—and then we went and had banana splits at the town's ice cream shop. It was about a mile and a half away from school, so fairly close to home as well. Now this may all sound corny to you, but it worked. I was 15 and I won over the best girl that had laid on the earth. Me. I got her. And then I lost her. But I had her. I had her and I should have never let her go, but I guess that's just what I'm good at, huh? Ruining people's lives.

MONDAY, SEPTEMBER 17TH, 1973

Another birthday that I could've gone without. It was the opening day of Lynn's Petals, and to be honest I have no clue why I thought opening it on that specific day was a good idea. I guess I thought since it was named after Mama, it should've opened on the day of her death, like a memorial or something to her. I had hoped that it'd be a great day and it would be a smashing success with hundreds of people coming in and ordering flowers. I wanted to do something that could make Mama proud, but of course it wasn't a hit. I'm pretty sure no one even knew the building was being used for something. I mean it had been closed for god knows how long. And it was next to a bar for crying out loud! What drunk buys flowers? None that I ever knew of.

Anyway, that morning I walked to the shop at 8 AM, went inside, and set up for the day. I had a front counter with a money drawer, a typewriter for typing poetry to pass the time, and a calculator. I also had a fan in there cause I didn't have the air set at too cold of a temperature. I thought it might kill the flowers, and besides, I didn't want to pay the extra money. I had four white tables, all of different sizes and heights, spread in the four corners of the room. One had roses on it that I had bought from Mr. Brady's because I just needed something to fill the table up. One had tulips on it that I stole from one of the graves at the yard a few nights before, and the third table had carnations from Sal's on it.

Hopefully no one from Sal's came into the shop because they'd be in for a rude awakening. The last table had poppies on it that I plucked from the garden in the back. They were all in different arrangements, but nothing too plentiful. I just didn't have enough flowers... not even enough for a dozen. Someone could buy one, three, five, or a half dozen of flowers. One was 25 cents, three were 50 cents, five were $1, and six were $1.50. I had all of the prices handwritten in a tiny pamphlet, like a menu at a restaurant.

The violet walls really looked wonderful; it added happiness into the room and made it a comfortable place to be in. I turned my closed sign around at 9 AM and propped the door open with a flower pot and waited. Waited for nobody to come, that is. When two o'clock hit, and not even one passerby had stopped in to look at my shop, I pretty much gave up. A few minutes after I closed the doors, I glanced through the front window at a tall figure dressed in all black. He was just standing there, motionless, hiding his face.

I swiftly walked towards the door to let him in when he swung his right arm out and before I could even think, the front window shattered before my very face. The man calmly turned—and walked away. I was so startled that I didn't even do anything about it. I didn't chase after the dark-shadowed man, I didn't call the police because I actually didn't have a phone set up yet at the store. I just laid there, staring at my hopes and dreams shattered on the floor in front of me, and disappointingly said, "Happy Birthday, Graham."

Graham Embry Soyle
10/15/06

ROSE

Love and Romance

*I**t took me a long time to find out why my father started drinking.*** I used to think about it for long periods of time, ya know: think about what went wrong and if I was the cause of it. Perhaps Mama cheated and he found out and started drinking his sorrows away and beating her out of anger.

I never saw Mama as a liar or a sneak. I never saw Mama as being a bad person, but yet I still had no explanation for Paul's outbursts. He used to be "Dad," until he changed of course. Then I called him who he really was: Paul, a beater, a drinker, a coward, and a *prick*. Never did cheat as far as I'm aware though, so maybe he had an ounce of loyalty left in him. But I doubt it.

There used to be a glass vase that rested upon the mantel-piece above the fireplace, and inside that vase lay withered away a brown rose. It was so dried out and discolored, I never would have known it was a rose if it wasn't for the story that went with it.

TUESDAY, MARCH 18TH, 1975

A dreary day at the graveyard. A lot had happened since I opened the flower shop, but it was all positive. First and foremost I hired an employee. His name was David. I had put up a couple flyers around town that I was looking for someone to help out at the shop part-time. Within a couple days I had four applications to look through and set up interviews with, two of which didn't even show and the third girl was borderline psychotic, so I ended up going with David. He seemed like a good guy; hard worker. He was in his 20s and was just trying to get some extra cash to help pay for college so this was a perfect, easy job for him. The shop had been open for almost two years at that point, and business was booming.

How it worked was: I would stop by Murphy Creek in the morning before the shop opened and dig any holes that needed to be dug that day. Then, I would leave the graveyard unlocked for the day to allow people the opportunity to visit with their lost ones while I went to Lynn's Petals, opened it, and took down any orders that were requested. People could slip requests through the mail slot in the door if they wanted, or they could come by and request an order in person, or even call the phone that I finally had set up after six or so months of first being open. David would come in around 10 o'clock each day so that I could make the deliveries and still keep the shop open. I realized after the grand opening in 1973 that my business was not going to be like any other. Like Mr. Brady's, or like any other flower shop where customers come and browse around, pick out some that they like, and move on with their day. I would never have the supply for that sort of thing. So, I asked customers what they wanted, and assured them that I would try my best to get that particular flower arrangement for them in the next day or so.

Sometimes, I would even recommend a certain flower to them to try, especially if I knew I had that one available to me. I still had flowers set up around the building for those who did stumble inside, upon last moment's notice, to buy a dozen roses for their loved one or whatever the case. I would leave the shop around five or six, depending on the amount of orders that had been placed, and depending on how long it took me to make deliveries for that day, and I would head back to the yard where I would rake and tidy up the plots. I didn't allow David to deliver the arrangements because it was easier and quicker for me to do it, thanks to my paperboy days. Besides, delivering allowed me to get to know everyone in the town that I didn't know.

Sure, I missed the days when I would sit around all day and smoke cigarettes and talk to Bettie amongst the tombstones, but it was nice for a while to have a busy day with no time for a smoke break. That, of course, made the Doval I had after work even better than if I had been puffing on one all day long. I would lock and close up the gates, and then go right back inside, where I pulled out all the orders from that day at the shop. Most of them were easy, ya know; a half dozen alstroemerias, or one carnation. Some were harder to find, but I had a chart where I wrote down all the flowers that I spotted on the different plots around the yard, so I could always go back to the charts and search for the particular order. I had a system that worked for me and that no one knew about. David didn't even know where I got my flowers from, and frankly he didn't care. I was a successful business owner making enough money to live comfortably, and on top of that I only had one employee to pay, no car payment, no pet supplies to buy, no wife to support... sort of sad now that I think about it. But who cares? I was a man making his own money and keeping every penny of it.

My Mama would stare at that damn rose all the time. She would stop and stare almost every day, just for a moment, and then go back to her normal activities. There were times, however, that she would stop and stare for moments longer than her usual routine. These times were special to her, and I could tell because her eyes glistened with cheerful tears, despite the agonizing event she would endure during these special moments. Everytime Paul destroyed her face with his knuckles, it was as if Mama found peace in the dead petals of that blessed rose. She would look straight through the blood and tears of her pain and find happiness in the flower. I wish I had her strength, I wish I had the power to fight off pain in that way. But unfortunately and strangely enough I am more like Paul than I am my Mama...

There I was on my bicycle, pedaling towards Lynn's Petals. Pedaling, petals, peddling... Interesting! So many different pedals. Anyways, I had all of the orders for the next day in the bag around my shoulders. I would go to the flower shop again after I locked up the graveyard because I wanted to get everything set up for the next day of business. I would wrap the flowers up in bunches with tissue paper and rubber bands, making sure to clip the thorns off of any roses or thorny species before wrapping them up. Then I would staple a piece of paper with the total amount due, the customer's name, phone number, and address to the tissue paper. Sometimes, the buyer of the flowers wrote a little message with the order for their significant other or whoever so I made sure to include those as well.

Usually, I made it home around eight o'clock at night, where I would whip up some dinner for myself, smoke three or four cigarettes to catch up from the busy day, and pass out in bed, where I would then wake up the next morning just to repeat the exact same bullshit from the day before. Don't get me wrong; I loved my new lifestyle, but I wonder why I even did it sometimes. I didn't have anybody I needed to support, so why work so much? To pass the time? To fill up the empty holes in my life? Husbands work three jobs to take care of their wives and their children, but I just worked because I was bored and had nothing else in life. It makes me sad to think about.

Thursday, December 15th, 1960

I'll never forget when I was 14 and I had just come home from school. It was a frosty December afternoon, and I ran through the front door, excited because there was only one more day of school before the holiday vacation. My excitement went away when I walked into Paul holding Mama's neck, squeezing tighter and tighter with each second. I always tried to stop him from hurting her but I never succeeded—I was too lanky— and I always just made him angrier. I watched as Mama glimpsed above the fire to the beaten down rose hidden behind glass and smiled. Paul finally had had enough of her enjoying her punishment, so he reached up, grabbed the flower vase, and smashed it over her head.

He then proceeded to retrieve the rose from the floor and rip every petal off individually, shove them into his mouth, chew for about eight seconds, and spit them up on Mama's face. She didn't even look like she was in pain from the broken glass on her head. She just looked distraught, like she had lost her entire life in a quick minute. A few weeks later, I asked Mama about the flower.

I wanted to know what it meant to her for her to be so upset about losing it. Whimpering, Mama told me, "Graham, your father wasn't always this way. He used to be kind, g-good. He used to love me. The reason I cared so much for that precious rose was because it was the only thing I had left to hang on to from your father's good days. He gave that beautiful, deep red flower to me on our third dating anniversary, along with an engagement ring.

We were so young and in love we didn't even care about rushing into anything. I kept the rose in a vase, watched it die, and never took it out. It may have been an ugly, smelly, brown collection of petals to most people who saw it, but to me it symbolizes love and hope. After Paul started drinking and getting angry with me, I would look at that flower when I needed to be reminded of hope and great things in life, and every time I looked at it my pain went away. I was rushed back into memories of my life when things were pure and God was good to me. And n-now I have n-nothing to stop the pain, n-no way of remembering w-what used t-to be. And that, Graham, is what that precious rose meant to me." Little did I know at the time that the father figure she was describing as being this wonderful man to her was not even Paul Soyle.

I arrived home around 8:20 PM on March 18th, 1975, reheated some leftover turkey and green beans from the night before, and then reached for my pack to retrieve my cigarettes. What I found inside the bag was not just a pack of cigarettes and some lighter fluid, but one single, red, thornless, rose. It was just about the most beautiful rose I had ever seen in my life, with five rows of petals and a stem the color of freshly-mowed grass in the spring. I must've missed it when I sorted the orders out that night, but for some reason that rose came home with me that night, and I didn't think twice about it. I filled up a tall vase full of water and placed the rose inside it and upon the mantlepiece in my living room. I guess I thought of it as a replacement for Mama's because she never was the same after she lost it. I'm sorry Mama, I never meant for anything bad to happen to you.

Graham Embry Soyle
10/20/06

JABOROSA

BEAUTY AND GRACE

SUNDAY, MARCH 18TH, 1982

I *decided it was time to get a new haircut.* I had sort of let my hair do its own thing ever since the whole River event happened so it had grown to be pretty long. I just didn't care enough about anything, especially about scheduling an appointment at the barber, so my locks started to look like a spitting image of the rest of my life: convoluted and useless.

River's birthday was coming up if I remember correctly... March 17th. Yeh that's right! St. Patrick's Day, too. Her looming birthday that she was not going to get the chance to celebrate that year was stressing me out and made me reevaluate every decision I ever made in life. River always took care of keeping up with my hair and she always made sure it looked neat and proper. Deciding it was time for new things, I went crazy and asked Cindy at the barber shop for a perm that day. I hated what it looked like, but I thought it fit my personality better than an immaculately coiffed head.

Plus, it made me resemble Ted, and I wanted to be more like him at the time. Speaking of acting more like Ted... ya know Cindy, the hairdresser... well, she was just idiotic. Plain and simple. Just no common sense at all. However, she was really nice and she had these adorable little dimples in her cheeks. After she finished executing the puff of fur on my scalp, she spritzed about 10 sprays of this clear liquid on it and leaned in closer to my head, whafting the smells into her nostrils as she proceeded to say, "Mmmm, smells like freshly plucked flowers."

Her dimples almost completely disappeared as she saw my smile turn into a frown. "What is your favorite flower, Cindy?" I politely asked her. "Oh, my! I just love daisies. I love the colors of them and their shape. Daisies are definitely my favorite. Too bad I'm deathly allergic to them... even the sight of them will make my throat close up. What's your favorite?"

Well let's just say lil' miss Cindy answered that question incorrectly and it cost her a potentially steep tip. Oh, and also her life. But the barber shop was crowded that day and it would have been a little too obvious as to how she died, so I faked it for a little while longer. Patience is worth it, trust me. I did the only thing I could do and asked her on a date for that night.

Around seven o'clock that night I went back to the barbershop to pick up Cindy after her shift was finished. She wanted to go to some Italian restaurant on the other side of town, but unfortunately for her, she wasn't going to make it that far. I ended up driving us to an unknown (well, not very known) forested area right outside of town, where I had rigged my passenger door to where it could only be opened from the outside, hence no room for escape.

It wasn't til about 20 minutes into the drive that poor Cindy caught on to the fact we weren't heading to the Italian place of her choosing. "Oooh a surprise! I really wanted Chef Carmici's homestyle spaghetti and meatballs... but I'm interested to see what you've chosen to satisfy me tonight," she stated, with a sensual ring to it if I may add.

When I literally didn't even look at her direction when she said that, she started to get flustered. I could see her from the corner of my eye. I think panic really began when she noticed my "driving gloves." She started screaming and kicking her feet against the windshield, while I just kept driving silently; I knew she wasn't strong enough to break it.

The forest was extremely dense so I had to turn my high beams on. Well one of them actually (the right one was out), and within minutes of doing so a giant deer appeared in front of us and refused to move. BAM! We crashed. The windshield was certainly shattered at that point. I looked over and Cindy was crawling out the little back window into the truck bed. Hmm I suppose I didn't think that one through. I had been strapped in by a crushed-in door from swerving and hitting a tree a few miles back and I wasn't able to move as quickly as I needed to.

After I had finally pried myself out from under my seatbelt, Cindy had already escaped, so I was on the search. I knew she couldn't have ran far, seeing as she didn't have a flashlight like myself, so I just ran around until I found her. She was hiding behind a nearby tree when I struck her with my calloused fist (I wasn't quite ready to kill her yet); I just needed her to stop moving. I had brought some thick rope with me to tie her against the tree whilst I did my work.

I wanted this kill to be a statement, a warning that there was indeed a serial killer on the loose. With my signature leather gloves still on, I slowly started removing her clothes... I wanted to remember this one. She had several tattoos; I remember that in full detail. I admired that really—it wasn't a very common thing at the time. She had a tattoo on her ankle of a crescent moon, with the phrase "Love you to the Moon and Back" written in what looked like handwritten cursive around the crescent of the moon, so that the words followed the shape of the picture entirely. She also had one on the back of her neck of a heart with the name Tristian written inside. Her son perhaps? Her husband? Never did find out to be honest with you. With her bare body trapped to the side of the tree, she finally started to gain back her consciousness. To keep her quiet, I had already stuffed her mouth and taped it closed with the orange headscarf that she was wearing.

I enjoyed watching her mascara-filled tears run down her bruised cheeks. She knew exactly what was about to happen, and that was satisfying enough. When I was at her salon earlier I had slipped a pair of her scissors into my pocket for that very moment. I started by cutting off all of her hair. I needed to strip her of all dignity and give her a taste of what she did to people everyday. Then I engraved G.E.S. right below her collarbone and proceeded to stab her in the stomach. I worked my way back up to her bald head and shoved the knife into her left eye. I watched her writhe in pain for a while and then I performed surgery on her other eye. I wanted people to find her tied to the tree, find her so brutally attacked, find her with MY initials engraved into her body. I wanted to leave my mark, to leave a warning. A warning to stay away from Graham Embry Soyle and a warning to never even smile at the thought of a daisy. That was the plan anyway... before I was so rudely interrupted I sliced half of her tongue off with my dull knife and watched the blood pour out through her lips.

Right as I was about to take her final breath, I heard voices and they were close by. "Heellloo? Hello! Do you hear that? Hellooo who's out there?" a man and a woman shouted. At the sound of the first "hello" I had to leave Cindy tied to that tree. I had to save myself. I started to panic as I wondered what would happen if she remembered my name, or identified me in a photo. G.E.S. would be over in no time. I started running around frantically questioning my next move, when all of a sudden I realized just how smart I was.

That woman was now only capable of performing two out of the five senses, and they're the two least important ones. She may know who committed this terrible crime but she'll have no way of communicating it. I felt bad for her in a way. I mean I never meant for her to suffer horrifically; I was planning on ending her misery for her. I jumped in my truck and skidded in the opposite direction of the chaos, beheading several trees in my path.

As I was shredding through the dense trees, I heard the sirens. I saw the blue and red, blinding, terrifying lights. I knew at that moment that they had found her. My plan had fallen into place! A little screwy in some areas, but the final outcome was all that mattered. MY initials were finally going to be the talk of the town! "WHO IS G.E.S?" I could see it as the headline for the paper the next day. I made a clean break out of the woods before any policeman saw me and I drove straight home. I knew I had to have an alibi. I just had no idea what it was going to be at the time. Although I knew my big reveal was on the horizon, I wasn't truly prepared for myself to get so carried away that night, so I was frantic to say the least. Let's just say late March 14th, early March 15th was a very long, grueling, hectic period of time for me. I had to think quickly and make smart decisions, which we all know I was never really good at.

The Lake of Wishes and myself met again that night. That's right. The Lake of Wishes had turned into Graham's Lake of Secrets and I liked it. The chances of the cops tracing those tire marks to my vehicle were high, so good ol' Louis had to go deep down to the bottom of the lake, where Bettie would keep him company. I had a lot of great memories in Louis, memories that you all will never understand.

Louis was passed down from Mama and was one of the only things I had left of her after she died. He kept me company through many lonesome rides. Hell he even landed me smack damn on the outskirts of Meerdin! He knew great things would come from that town... And need I forget to mention his courageous assistance in my everlasting infamous crimes.

I had a real heart-to-heart that night at the lake's dirty edge... with Louis, with Bettie, with River, with myself. It was good for me. I needed it. It was strange how I killed him... it wasn't your average everyday car death. I parked him at the lake like it was any normal moonlit night and proceeded to have my heart-to-heart, or my eulogy in a sense *before* the death. It was nice that way; it felt like he was a part of it. When I was ready, I hopped inside and started him up, muted the radio because I felt like the loud noise would have ruined the moment, and then reversed a good 20 feet.

I pushed the gas pedal as far as it would go that night and floated above the lake for about half a second before splashing loudly into the murky, lukewarm water. It was one of the most incredible experiences I ever had. The car was sinking very slowly, so for a good seven or eight minutes, I was floating on top of the water, staring out the window at the night sky, experiencing a moment of pure bliss.

As soon as that blissful period was over, I realized the intensity of the situation I was in and started to replay the events of that night in entirety. All was good, all was how it should be...until... until it hit me like a tornado.

I may have taken Cindy's seeing and speaking capabilities away from her, but I left her completely free to write MY name, draw MY face, reveal MY identity on any piece of paper near her. "How could I be so stupid?" I thought. "I finally made a mistake, I finally slipped up somewhere...this is it..."

But I couldn't just give up and leave the town I had made so much progress in. I couldn't just run, like my good-for-nothing father. I couldn't abandon my graveyard or Lynn's Petals... Mama would be so disappointed in me. The only choice I had was to fix my mistakes and eliminate the problem once and for all. Not sure how I slept that night, but I decided to sleep in my office at the yard, just in case she revealed the identity of her torturer that very early morning. After just a few winks, I gathered a bunch of jaborosas that I planned on delivering to an elderly woman that afternoon, and pedaled fast towards the city bus station, where I would just happen to catch the first bus to Dover City Hospital. This was risky business, but I claimed to have seen the policemen and ambulances speeding away when I was coming home from work the night before. Reaching out as a nice citizen, I wanted to bring flowers to whoever the unlucky soul aboard that ambulance was. Buying my story entirely, and even appreciating it, I was allowed visitor access.

There I was. At the foot of my victim's bed. And I couldn't believe it. I couldn't believe how lucky I was. She was in a coma. I acted as if I was extremely distraught over the paused life of such an innocent, beautiful soul and started sobbing my best "fake tears." And that is what started my daily ritual of coming to the Dover hospital to visit Cindy, eventually with the plan to cut off her air supply—doing her in for good—but for the time being I had to take myself off of the suspect list.

Skipping forward a couple weeks, I began to become tired of keeping up this fake persona, so I decided to end it once and for all. Since she loved daisies so much, why not let the daisy itself kill her? I gathered two dozen fresh daisies from Samantha Syprett's headstone and started on my final journey to visit my victim.

After her tragedy, the town of Meerdin took pity on Cindy and soon she became the talk of the town, along with her mysterious attempted murderer, G.E.S., so it was a common occurrence for random civilians to visit her in her time of unconsciousness. I had become a friendly face at the reception's desk at that point, so I just gave a friendly wave as I walked past the desk to Room 314, Cindy's suite. Little did they know... I was G.E.S. muahahaha! No one was in the room at the moment, but there were bunches of balloons and cards and roses all over the place, so I knew people had been there already that day.

I placed the bouquet of two dozen daisies on her chest, with her hands clasping the stems, making sure her nose was basically pressed right up against the petals. I lowered the sound on the machines in the room, and stood back and stared. She truly looked beautiful laying there. What a shame. I knew I had to get out of there before she went into anaphylactic shock and flatlined so I swiftly walked past the reception desk, shouting "see you tomorrow!" as I left.

SATURDAY, MARCH 17TH, 1979

River's first birthday that we celebrated together where I planned a night out bowling. That was her favorite pastime, even though she was awful at it. I always tried to let her win when we went, but it was so hard because of how competitive I've always been. I never could control my competitiveness to allow her to win, but I did try to play nice at the beginning... until I couldn't handle it anymore.

That night she twisted her ankle trying to do some fancy leg swing when she went to throw the ball towards the end of the last round, so then we went to the arcade part of the building and played some games for the rest of the night, sipping on soda, laughing the night away. It was a great time. The bowling alley had everything decorated in green colors for the holiday and they had a costume contest and discounted food and drinks. Good memories… I miss her.

I recall the next morning after bowling very vividly because we woke up to a random snow storm; it was beautiful. I loved the snow because it made me feel like I was in a wonderland away from the reality I didn't want to be in. We stayed inside all afternoon watching movies cuddled up on the couch. Her favorite was *The Sound of Music* and mine was *Rear Window*. Then when it hit around dinner time and the snow had slowed down, we decided to go get a couple burgers at Sal's. Dawn wasn't there that night, and of course the dumbass replacement waitress messed up my usual order and smothered my plate with ketchup. I could've killed her right then and there, only I realized I was in a public place and I wasn't quite ready to go to prison just yet.

MONDAY, SEPTEMBER 17TH, 1979

I guess since I told you about her first birthday together, I could tell ya about mine. She wanted so badly to give me a great first birthday together, but as everybody knows, I hate my birthday (she just didn't know that yet). First, she woke me up with breakfast already made (there's nothing I hate more than eating as soon as I wake up; I'm not hungry!) then she tells me she has a day planned full of surprises and that she had already called David and told him not to come in and to reschedule the deliveries for the next day. *Great.*

So after being forced to eat at the crack of fucking dawn, she drags me out the door on some several hour-long drive to BFE (Bum Fucking Egypt). Cause that's what I want to do on my birthday, spend it sitting in a car... yeh right. No! So then we arrive to some brewery, which I'll admit was very historic looking and interesting, but... I would have been even more happy enjoying a beer on my couch in my undies. But women don't get that, do they? They spend so much time trying to make you happy that they don't realize all we want to do is sit around and be lazy. Especially on our birthdays!

That wasn't the end either... after spending too much money on craft beer, we then had to drive hours to get back to Meerdin, just to end up at some way-too-fancy restaurant just to spend even *more* money. I mean whose idea was it to think it's a fun time to go broke on your birthday? I enjoy her efforts, but I didn't enjoy the day at all. She tried too hard.

I don't enjoy being locked in a small box with nowhere to go. I miss being able to take my evening walks with Gene, smokin' a cig and chuggin' a beer. Man are those days long gone... It was the little things, ya know? I mean who invented time anyway? And why did they make it go by so fast? It doesn't make any sense to me. The beginning, the middle, the end. It'd be so much easier if it were never discovered. No one would ever worry about being on time to dinner, or scheduling a meeting, or making someone eat at a certain hour, or picking a date to kill someone, or dwelling on the day that you might kick the bucket, or (insert a million other examples). It's just crazy to me. Why did someone do that to us? Why not just keep letting us cavemen live the way we were living; day to day, without worry. But no! Now everything has a date! A time! A limit! And it's causing everyone to go crazy, and I'm sick of it!

Speaking of times and dates and stuff, I don't think I ever

told you about Scotty and Sabrina's proposal. It was spring of 1972 and Scotty finally worked up the nerve to ask her to spend the rest of her life with him. I remember him asking me to go with him to pick out a ring. He didn't have much money at the time so I lent him some so he wouldn't show up with a dinky little thing. We probably went to seven different pawn shops around town before he found one he thought she'd like. It was gold with a red ruby stone on it cause it was her favorite color. Later that night he took her to the most expensive Italian restaurant in town and performed the most cliché proposal anyone could think of—put the ring in her champagne glass. But, it worked for 'em. They decided to get married in the winter; her idea, not his.

I didn't much care for Sabrina—she was really needy and took up all of Scotty's time. I hardly ever got to hang out with him anymore. I never really saw him with a person like that; he's so independent and never liked having to take care of someone else. But they ended up doing pretty well I guess, for as long as they lasted at least.

Tuesday, October 31st, 2006

Tired of me yet? I sure am. Go on, set it down and come back to it later. You need a break too. Besides, they say it's dinner time.

Graham Embry Soyle

10/31/06

PSYCHOTRIA ELATA

Sex and Lust

They call me Luna cause I'm a lunatic
I'm a double-sided conundrum that can slaughter you
My mind continuously echoes the disappointment I've become
Every whisper becomes
Every regret becomes
Every step becomes
Every image...
Pictures on walls aren't pictures at all
Pictures are just lost souls stuck on Mars
Put together from past and present sorrows
Pictures of flowers bleed yellow stains down the back of my head
I can't get rid of any of it.
Every feeling, every touch, every piece of you
Every longing, every desire, every piece of me
Every haunting laughter that wishes to be
Nothing
But with them
I can't escape.

Thursday, November 9th, 2006

orry, I tend to be pretty bored here most of the time. I used to write poetry as a teenager, but then I started having to work and take care of Mama, then the whole fleeing to Delaware thing happened, then I became pretty busy for a while trying to find myself, and then losing myself again of course. But for some reason when I woke up this morning, I had this burning urge to express myself. This has been the first time I've ever even *thought* about writing again, let alone actually doing it. Kinda nice feeling, ya know.

When I was younger I used to try to make up stories of why I was even alive. I didn't understand why, if my dad didn't love me, why was I there? He hurt my mother, he hurt me— why did they bother bringing me into this world? But then at the age of 18, I found out exactly why Paul hated us.

When the boy was three,
His father long gone; he asked his mother, who lay beside him reading a bedtime story, "Mommy, what are those lines on your wrists?"

She told him, "I don't want to scare you, but when you were born, pirates tried to take you and left marks when they attacked me!"
Satisfied, the boy looked up at his mother, a warrior, with magic in his heart and awe in his eyes.

When the boy was six,

Just starting school; he asked his mother who stood beside him admiring his newest crayon masterpiece, "Mama, the other kids said pirates aren't real. What are those marks on your wrists?"

She told him, "You're right, I didn't want to scare you. When you were born, a vampire tried to take you, and it left scars when it attacked me!"
Content, the boy looked up at his mother, a vampire slayer, with curiosity in his heart and wonder in his eyes.

When the boy was twelve,
Almost a young man, he asked his mother who leaned over him helping him with his homework,
"Mama, vampires are just made-up stories, so why are there scars on your wrists?"
She told him "You're right, I didn't want to scare you. When you were born, an enemy spy tried to take you and attacked me when I wouldn't let him!"
Inspired, the boy looked up at his mother, a hero, with courage in his heart and pride in his eyes.

When the boy was eighteen,
He stumbled through the door drunk, and said to his mother who sat staring at an old photo,
"I know the truth, I know what those scars are on your wrists."

She told him, "You're right, I didn't want to scare you. When you were born, your father was driving to the hospital because I went into labor. You were coming! Our precious baby was coming! In the quick of the night, and the slickness of the rainy streets, he crashed. Your real father. Crashed. I couldn't stop blaming you. You took him away from me and all I wanted was to see him again."

Broken, the boy looked down at his mother, a woman, with nothing in his heart and sadness in his eyes.

He wasn't my dad—that poor excuse of a man—wasn't my father. He wasn't my blood. It's all a big lie. I remember when I first found out that night. I was so happy that I wasn't related to that horrible man. I was happy that I didn't have to worry about turning into him. But then why is it that I am so much like him? I've done terrible things in my life, just like Paul Robert Soyle. I think once you're around someone for so long, you can't help but become them.

My Mama told me more about my birth father over the next few years and how she moved on and it was heartbreaking. His name was Keith Laverne Windom, born and raised in Wichita. He and my Mama met when she was 18, he was 20, and he was on leave for a few days from the war. They met in a small bar called Picadilly's. Supposedly, their eyes locked in the middle of "Crazy He Calls Me" that was blaring from the corner jukebox, and that is why it was always her favorite song.

She never went too much into detail about the love they shared or the more intimate moments they had, but she told me that their feelings for each other were unlike no other. I believed her. The way she talked about him, I could tell she loved him very much. Her expression changed when she would tell me about how she met Paul and how she was unfaithful to her true love. She looked guilty. She claimed she was lonely with Keith being at war. She met a man by the name of Paul in 1944, who sat the war out to take care of his widowed mother, and she spent most of her days with him. Apparently, she went with both men for a year, managing to not tell either one about the other, until of course, the war ended, and Keith came home. She told Paul she couldn't see him again, which she stood by. She was with Keith's child, and she said she was never happier.

Her water broke on the 16th of September, late at night, and my birth father rushed to the hospital in a little red truck. Only, he never made it to the hospital. Not alive, anyways. A station wagon slammed into the driver's side going 40 mph and his heart stopped instantaneously. Mama says we almost didn't make it either, but doctors said it was a miracle. I guess she blamed me. She blamed me for his death, for Keith's death. If she had never gone into labor, then Keith never would have rushed to the hospital, and he never would have been killed. That's why she slit her wrists I guess—she felt guilty and wanted to punish herself for blaming the death of her true love on the birth of her only son. When asked to sign the birth certificate when I was born, she wrote my name down as Graham Embry Soyle, so I guess she had made her choice to lie to Paul and tell him I was his.

She told me she went back to Paul cause she needed someone to share her life with and she needed a man's support for her new baby and herself. At first, Paul made her forget about the loss of her beloved Keith and life was good and moving in a forward direction. He was bursting with joy at the fact that he had a son... until...

Paul eventually found out that she had an affair and that

would be when the drinking started. He started beating her out of anger and she took it because she thought it was the appropriate punishment for herself. Like the cutting, I guess. She felt the need to punish herself for just a stupid mistake! Paul never looked at me the same after he found out I wasn't his; basically disowned me.

Like I give a fuck... I mean I don't blame him for hating me sometimes. He had a son, and then he didn't in the blink of an eye, but he would have responded differently. He could've made do with what he was given. I mean, he raised me... He was technically my father. I think the only reason he stayed with us is because he liked having control over Mama and me. He probably took pity on us, too. Well now you know why my father was an asshole. Still no excuse but at least there's a reason for it all.

TUESDAY, JUNE 10TH, 1975

A strange day. A lanky, young reporter by the name of Fred came to Lynn's Petals and asked the most bizarre question. "Do you have any psychotria elata?" he asked me. I had never heard of that flower before, and I was so embarrassed because I looked like an idiot when I responded. To this day, I still never found one of those flowers to put in my book. Anyways, the reporter shrugged it off and started talking to me about his column assignment. He was so excited cause I guess this was his first column or something. He showed me his rough draft, titled **Meerdin's Missing Members,** and asked me if I knew any information that might be beneficial to his research.

Meerdin's Missing Members
With such a small population, it doesn't take much for the good people of this town to start realizing that residents are dropping like flies. Twenty-one people have gone missing since January 1st of last year, and three have been missing for up to six years now and people are starting to question the safety of their once-beloved town. Police are investigating the situation further, but please report any information to the local police station and send love and hope towards the families of those still looking for their missing loved ones. **Missing: Bettie Murphy, Daisy Dahlman, Spencer Buchanan, Nichole Sanders, Jeffrey Cobb, Roy Barker, Amy Vaughn, Lindsay Mendez, Shannon Sepessy, Gilberto Hughes, Carla McGee, Leslie Casey, Misty Maynard, Alexandria Simone, William Simone, Digna Ochoa, Brent Gentry, Linette Valenti, Selena Vessel, Carl Peterson, Violet Griffin**

SATURDAY, DECEMBER 2ND, 2006

I've always wanted to experience something traumatic and live to tell the tale, ya know? Like something out of an action movie where you get kidnapped or lost at sea. How amazing would it be to be kidnapped from a gas station and locked in somebody's trunk? I've been imagining a scenario like this for the longest time, since I was a kid. *My kidnapper would drive down busy roads on the highway and I would have no way of knowing where they were taking me, but I still try to take as many mental notes as I can until my kidnapper stops quickly and tosses me in a field of 10-foot corn. My faceless kidnapper then starts chasing me through the mazes of corn with a knife until my adrenaline takes over my body and I outrun him and escape with only a few scrapes and a wonderful story.* Maybe I'm the only person who feels this way, but I just want something exciting to happen to me. Ya know how kids always fantasize of unicorns and rainbows and use their imagination to create a perfect world for them to live in? Well, I was always the kid, and still am the kid, that drew up ideas of getting locked in trunks. Psychotic? I don't think so. I like to say imaginative.

Graham Embry Soyle
12/02/06

SATURDAY, JUNE 25TH, 1983

My dear friend forced me to be admitted into a psych ward, or as the government likes to refer to them, an "Institution for the Mentally Unstable." Good ol' Scotty... said I wasn't myself anymore. He manhandled me into his car, drove me there himself, and dragged me to the check-in window. He was kind enough to explain that I was just dog-drunk and having suicidal thoughts, when he could've just told them the truth and had me locked up for good. It was about 45 minutes outside of Dover and the entire car ride was just a long-ass lecture.

I never would have thought Scotty would've done that to me, although I suppose he just had my best interest at heart. Still, I felt so betrayed.

I wasn't crazy. After I told him, I expected him to be on board with what I was doing and join me. Everything I did was voluntary. It was what I wanted and enjoyed doing, and I just told him because he was my best friend. He just didn't understand me at all, not like I thought he did. I guess I couldn't really hold it against him; technically he was doing the right thing.

I just wish he would've chosen the better path. I don't know why he thought that place would help me anyways. He already thought I was crazy.

"Why not make Graham crazier by sticking him in a place full of crazies to talk about craziness?" is clearly what was going through his head when he made that decision. Merriwether Miracle House for the Institutionalized Insane was my home for a solid four weeks.

I wasn't mentally insane when I checked myself in by any means, but Jesus did that place drive me up the walls.

I remember meeting this girl named Gale when I was locked up in there. Now she was, by any definition, insane.

Everyone called her Gobbling Gale because she would make "gobble gobble" noises like a turkey on Tuesdays and Thursdays only. She made everyone refer to her as a turkey during those two days out of the week, and as a turkey trainer the other five days. She couldn't tell the difference between a fly on the wall and a fucking dragon. She just saw random shit and talked to it as if it were right in front of her.

But even as crazy as she was, she was still the least of the crazies there and definitely the only one there that I could bring myself to talk to. She may have imagined things but at least she had common sense. We ate lunch together and she even introduced me to her best friend, the frog, whom she never let anyone meet. So I felt pretty special. Besides, I needed *someone* to talk to. I couldn't be in that loony bin all alone.

I think I ended up spending around four weeks there before they finally realized I didn't need to be in there. It was just long days of a bunch of checkers and games of cards that I always lost at, and still suck at to this day. In a weird way, I sort of enjoyed my time there because it let me escape from my reality and experience the lives of strangers through other people's eyes.

Was an interesting experience for sure. At this current day, *if* Scotty could speak to me, I'd probably thank him for those miserable four weeks.

I guess I should explain why Scott can't actually speak to me anymore, even if he wanted to. The doctors at Merriwether called him when they decided to release me because he was the one who had me admitted, and he was my emergency contact, of course. So he comes to pick me up, greets me with a warm smile, signs the release paperwork, and congratulates me on healing myself or whatever. Something about my friend was unusual that day; I just didn't know what about him was so different. In the car, he talked to me a lot about what had been going on at the bar and in town.

He asked me many questions about my experience and if I was better. What really makes someone "better" anyway? What does that even mean?

I didn't think anything was wrong with me to begin with, so how was I supposed to become better by being surrounded by a bunch of nuts all day and having pointless conversations with "licensed medical professionals?" I thought the whole "psychiatric healing process" was bullshit and that's what I told Scotty.

He didn't like that answer. He kept talking to me like he didn't know me. He sounded almost like one of the shrinks I would have sessions with at the Miracle House. It became apparent to me that we were going the wrong way. We were headed out of Delaware entirely! He had been talking to me so much as a means of distracting me from the drive, and as soon as I caught on, he did something about it. He hit me in the head with his elbow two or three times, and that's all I remember. I blacked out. Makes me sad to think about... that my best friend would just abandon me on the side of the road in another state, hoping to never see me again. I'll finish this story later...

I remember being in love with this girl in the ward with us, Carolyn. She was like no one I had ever met before. Beautiful, crazy, enthusiastic, everything I could have ever asked for. We were perfect. But, we weren't. We exceeded the term "perfection" in every sense in our minds, but through an outsider's eye, we were far from the term. And everyone knew that. Except for us. Or at least me for that matter. Want to know what it feels like to be in love with someone whom you think/know is the one for you?

Well just be me. Cause that's my entire life. I'm really good at getting people to fall in love with me, but I've only truly been in love with one person in my life and that one person hasn't felt the same way about me. Well, I suppose that isn't entirely true; she loved me, but she was better than me, she didn't have the holdbacks that I did. She wasn't miserable every second of her life that she wasn't with me like I was with her. She doesn't know what it means to be without the one thing in her life that makes her wake up in the morning willing to live. She will never have to endure that part of life. And good for her. I hope she never has to. But who wishes for me? No one. And that's the issue. Who is there for me? When am I going to be the person that someone thinks about? Will I ever be? I'm not too sure. And I'm not sure that I will ever be.

But that's okay. I'd rather be a nobody than be someone that a person cannot stop thinking about. I don't want to break anyone's heart. I am here to tear hearts out, not just wound them.

I want to tell you what I am feeling but I can't because at this point, nothing I say means anything to you anyway, so what's even the point? I don't know, so why even bother? You will just disregard it anyway. But you still glare over at me and ask me what's on my mind (even though you don't care), and I look over at you and tell you *nothing* even though we both know that's a lie. We still look into each other's eyes and accept it because even if you *wanted* to know, you don't. And even if I *wanted* to tell you, I don't. And we have both come to that sad understanding. We deal with it. And we move on. And that's that. I'm tired of being a menace.

Cell mate problems, am I right?

Graham Embry Soyle
12/02/06

ALSTROEMERIAS

FRIENDSHIP, LOVE, STRENGTH, AND DEVOTION

FRIDAY, OCTOBER 7TH, 1977

day of remembrance. Seven years prior, poor Bettie sunk herself to the bottom of the lake, along with everyone else's wishes, and of course no one found her body because no one cared enough to really look, and other than Gene, I was the only one who knew the truth.

It was time for her to have a proper burial service, even though it was almost identical to the ceremony she had before. The only thing missing was a woman by the name of Iris, Bettie's friend that worked at the department store on East Berman Street.

Iris herself passed away sometime in that seven-year span. Sad, but not really missed to tell you the truth. The state of Delaware must have noticed me somehow because I received a visit after her funeral from two men in suits. We had an informal meeting in my office that basically stated that all of Bettie's property and belongings went straight to the state because she had no family to claim it and she had no will. Little did they know, I had a will from Bettie herself in my pocketbook at all times.

Obviously I couldn't show these suited men this crinkled piece of paper, for it would've changed her whole case to a suicide case and I may have also been incriminated for keeping information from the law. So, my mouth stayed shut.

Luckily, she had no money to give to the state because she didn't believe in banks and she had already given me the money with her third key.

The suited men had some questions for me about how the graveyard was managed and the steps that I take on an everyday basis, so I told them. I mentioned that Vern was my paid employee, and that he helped out regularly, which was a little white lie because all he really did was help me lower caskets into the ground.

Anyways, I mentioned that Meer Murphy Creek was family owned and I wanted to stick with the system that I was introduced to, which involved a rule that families are not allowed to stay and view the lowering of the casket or the final burial process of covering the casket with dirt.

They can come and see the casket in the ground for their service, but the process of watching it happen was forbidden. I'm not sure why the Murphy's set that regulation, but I never had an issue with people complaining about it.

I opened the gates, dug graves for the individuals that I knew were being dropped off from different funeral homes and local morgues, scheduled the burial services and ceremonies with the families, tended to the yard, and handled the finances. They saw how invested I was in the graveyard so they offered it to me first before they put it on the market for sale. Also lucky.

No one knew I was living in her home though, therefore it was foreclosed and put on the market one month later. Not so lucky. I bought Murphy Creek from the state of Delaware for $9,575.00. That money came out of Bettie's small fortune, of course, but I hardly had any left, considering I already bought the space for Lynn's Petals out of this lump sum as well.

This was a huge risk for me because it left me with no money to fall back on, but I really had no option other than to purchase the graveyard. Bad bad things may have happened if someone else got ahold of that yard.

The night after the suited men left my office, I went to Sal's for the first time in two years. I looked for 20 minutes at every worker in that restaurant and for the life of me I could not find Dawn.

And then I finally saw her beautiful smile from across the room. She looked completely different. Her head was covered in this long, blonde hair and as soon as she saw me, she smiled from ear to ear. Two days later and I was living with her.

Living with Dawn was alright. I felt like I was living with somebody I didn't know and who I was never going to get to know.

We didn't talk—we didn't really even acknowledge each other. There was never any romance between us. It was downright boring.

I hated it, actually.

Another summer, another day
More and more pain, I must say
Why am I telling you this?
My words don't mean much
Anymore
But my thoughts
Are words unthought of
And they mean more and more
With every tear
With every tally mark
I shed my thoughts to you
To tell you
To confess my life to you
Although I cannot see the summer sun anymore
My thoughts of past regrets
Bring me home
Home once more

MONDAY, DECEMBER 18TH, 2006

You're probably wondering why I'm only telling you about my past. My past childhood, my past adulthood, my past life.

Let me show you a glimpse into my current life; not sure what kind of life it really is, so you'll be wishing I would've just stuck to my past, believe me. Whatever the case, this is my reality. These blank, cold, walls that look like white bricks but really are cheaply designed tiles, a mattress that is similar in size to one of those multi-colored mats you nap on in kindergarten, a metal toilet with an opening designed for accommodating a male mouse, and those freezing square-tile floors that are surprisingly more comfortable than my kindergarten mat some nights, despite the fact that they are as hard as bricks.

There are lots of different rooms here, even a courtyard, a dining hall, and a small church area! I like to classify it as my mansion, my mansion in the making. It's quite a shame I don't go to the church more often, considering it's the best room here, but ya know me and the whole church thing.

Me and the gods don't really get along. I mean, if God is real, why am I here? Why would He put me here as if this is my "path in life?" Please! It's all a sham. I tell Stickers every fucking day when he walks over there that he's wasting his damn energy.

Now I'm not gonna lie to y'all. I did go. Twice I've taken the after-dinner stroll to the white metallic-looking building with a pointed roof. Inside, there's two columns of benches, five rows wide each. A huge portrait of Jesus sits above the stage. The room full of peacefulness and dim lighting. And trust me I tried.

I tried to do what Stickers does and pray for mercy and pray to go to heaven. But every time I try, I can't get rid of the awful images that pass through my head, the images of how shitty my life was. I don't know, maybe I'm just not there yet. It's all a joke to me still, but unfortunately I don't have much time left to make friends with God.

The courtyard isn't your typical courtyard. It doesn't have

rows of perfectly mowed artistic grass pieces, it doesn't have stone gargoyles placed symmetrically around the area, and it certainly isn't a place one desires to go for a stroll, or to have a nice conversation. The courtyard I know is a place one fears. It's nicknamed the Fun Place ironically but the only people that have fun there are the men with power. The Fun Place is an outdoor concrete space, surrounded by wired fences and electrified sharp edges.

Absolutely no trees to provide shelter from the blistering Arizona heat waves. There is a basketball arena with two hoops, one on each end of the concrete slab, although neither of which has a net on it. Well, there used to be, until Jack was hanged from one last year. The powerful men felt that the nets were too dangerous and allowed opportunities for more of us to be hanged, so they took them away, just like everything else.

The mansion dining hall is a magnificent place to be, with hundreds of royal plastic chairs, and long, rectangular, stained folding tables. I even have my own crew of chefs that cook for me, and the entrees are always gourmet, and when I say gourmet I more so mean fancy, not-so-fancy, hot dogs that they slice in half just to make us feel like we're eating more food than we actually are, plus they taste like water with some partially frozen fries. If we even get fries.

It's typically some stale cornbread and, if we're lucky, some way-too-salty chips. HOWEVER, my chefs will sometimes save me their leftovers from home, maybe once or twice a month when I've been a decent person, which is pretty luxurious, even when the food is cold.

The bathroom is much bigger than a normal bathroom. It's

so big that it can fit 20 or so naked men at the same time! Walk-in showers, with water as cold as ice, and toilets similar to the one in my master suite.

The mirror was taken away after the whole "Jack and the Net" scene last year, but one of my buddies, Chex, happened to grab a piece of it before they took it down and sometimes he lets me look at it. It's hard to believe how old I am now and how gray my beard is. Funny, reminds me of how Vern looked when I last saw him.

I guess now is as good as any to start being more honest with you; you know most of my life now anyway. Remember the girl I told you that I had a one-night stand with? Yah, well, I vividly remember the sound of her soft lips that muttered the words, "Daisy Dahlman."

At first I smiled, but it wasn't exactly out of happiness; it was out of pure anger. An immediate flash of a memory from a night in my childhood where Paul came in holding three daisies and sitting them on the nightstand next to the recliner my mother was sitting in, asking for forgiveness for the dried blood and not-yet-purple bruises on her beautiful face. Just like he did every fucking time. How could he? And for that matter, how could SHE?

I heard that word, her name... Daisy... and I just snapped. Literally. I reached for her and just snapped her neck. It was so fast I hardly even knew what I was doing until it was too late. I was in a rage. All I saw was black and blue and then she was lying unconscious across the foot of the bed. What had I done? I had never had that kind of reaction before. Well, since my cow incident. But I was young; I thought I was over that. Apparently not. It was just the start.

So then it was time to figure out what I was going to do with her. How was I going to get her out of my house and to the graveyard to hide her with the other bodies? I had to act fast before someone remembered she had been with me that night, and also before she started to smell.

So I decided to just reverse my truck into the back yard and bring her out and slip her in the back. Just put my bags of trash on top of her and drove to the cemetery later that night. It was a lot easier than I thought actually. No one questioned me—it was my cemetery—so no one else was there to disturb me. I didn't even feel nervous throughout the process.

I went and I dug a hole six feet deep and one foot wide (she didn't need to be comfortable) in between two graves where I knew that no one else would have the chance of being buried because I always spaced the plots six feet apart from each other.

So, as long as she was in between two other plots, no one would ever find her, especially because I never wrote it in on my burial sheets. I stacked her inside and packed the dirt on top. It was a clean, smooth, naked grave of dirt. No tombstone means no evidence. Planted some seeds and grew the grass back in its place over time. Then I went home and slept like a rock.

SATURDAY, JUNE 4TH, 1977

I was walking home from work on my usual path, smoking a cigarette, when I spotted something strange out of the corner of my eye. It was poking out of the dirt on the right-hand side of the road. It was just sticking out, waiting for me to come and snatch it.

It was a woman's handkerchief, but I couldn't make out the design on it because it was so dirty and brown in color. I looked up from the handkerchief for a second and saw what seemed to be a path leading away from the road. I wanted to make sure there wasn't a woman in trouble somewhere so I carefully followed the marks in the dirt. They continued for what seemed like miles and before I even realized how long I had been walking, it was nighttime and I was standing in a moonlit forest of trees. Something that night kept me moving forward, although I probably should've stopped and turned back.

I came upon a small bridge, 10 feet long or so, that hung over a narrow, flowing creek. The bridge was very spooky, no doubt, with a slight mist that lay neatly over the top of the bridge about two inches above it. Everything about the atmosphere of that night told me to go home, but yet something kept drawing me in.

I felt like I was in a horror movie and it was my turn in the sequence to get killed. The sky was as dark as the deepest trenches of the ocean blue. The night was so quiet that I could hear my heart beating 80 beats per minute, and I kept checking behind me to see if my killer was approaching. This 10-foot bridge was made of deteriorating wood that had minor water damage and was covered with overgrown moss and vines.

The flowing creek below was only four feet or so from the bottom of the bridge, but there was a plethora of rocks awaiting my arrival at the bottom, so I didn't even dare put one toe on the base of that rickety old deathtrap. I called out a couple of times, asking if anyone was there, but I never heard a response. That was when I decided to sit down for a minute to catch my breath.

I barely did anything, but my adrenaline was working so hard, I felt like I had been running for a couple of miles. I remember thinking about life as I sat there and I still feel the same emotions now as I did then. It's so crazy how one can hate life so much and not give two shits whether one lives or dies, but when put into a situation like crossing a rickety old bridge, where life isn't guaranteed, one finds the joy in life and the desire to live another moment, at least past the moment of that bridge.

I decided to creep down the small bankside of the creek, carefully sliding down the rocks because I was thirsty. I was just about to lap up some water from the creek when I saw a white object caught up on a collection of rocks. After coming closer, I realized that it was a white blanket that was wrapped around an object no bigger than a cantaloupe. I reached my arm out as far as I could to try and grab it because it was in the middle of the rapidly flowing water, and I finally pulled it back into the bankside. I immediately froze when I saw what it was. I can still remember the shock I was in like I just pulled it out of the water for the first time again. A baby. A baby no older than one week or so.

A dead baby, blue in the face, colder than a brick of dry ice; ya know the cold that is so cold it burns you and makes you want to cry. He had some dried blood at the top of his head, so I rinsed the dirty handkerchief off in the water, and cleaned the blood off of his little head. Once the dirt was removed, I saw that the handkerchief was white in color, with yellow daisies lining the center of it, now with a brownish-red streak on it. Seems to be that daisies always bring death.

See, I have always had this habit of feeling guilty for things that happen, even though I had nothing to do with the situation at hand. Immediately, that's how I felt. I thought, "I killed this newborn baby," "I threw him off the bridge and left him for dead." I couldn't shake the feeling that I actually did it, so I sat there and mourned for a while, holding little Ron in my shaking arms. I made a whole story for Ron and the reason for his murder as a way of coping with the fact that I was a baby killer.

I convinced myself so well that night that sometimes still to this day, when I think about it, I have a hard time remembering that I *found* that poor baby dead. I *found* him upside down, blue-faced, and breathless in the creek. The sun started to come out in the distance, so I found the strength to get up off of the ground.

There was a rope ladder hanging from a tree beside the bridge, so I climbed up the ladder with baby Ron and found myself on the other side of the bridge from where I started. It was a strange open field of nothingness. Nothing but freshly-mowed grass and one sole tree in the center of the land with a wide trunk and beautiful lengthy branches, filled with blooming alstroemerias.

At the time, it felt like a fit place for Ron to spend his afterlife.

Looking back, I feel bad not laying him to rest in my own graveyard, but time was limited that morning, so I started to dig. I dug with my bare hands in the soft earth; one because I had no tools to assist me, and two because infants are required by law to be buried by hand, according to the state of Delaware. I could've reported it to the police, but that was just too much work at the time, and I tried to avoid cops at all costs for obvious reasons. Right under the alstroemerias he lay, along with the bloody handkerchief I placed in the hole with him.

Later on, I came back to place a proper headstone on his grave that read, "Here lies Ron the Bridge Baby. Short life, happy life. R.I.P." I returned every year for a while to replace his alstroemerias with fresh ones from the tree and every time I came to visit, the grass was always freshly mown. I never stole the flowers from that tree because I felt as if they belonged with the bridge, and the baby boy, and the mother that is burning in Hell, I'm sure.

FRIDAY, DECEMBER 15TH, 1978

The very first time that I ever flew on a plane. I was in my early 30s. It was Scotty's brother Steven's wedding and I was his plus one, even though normally I wouldn't give a shit about going to a wedding but I really just wanted to go see a new city. Sabrina couldn't get off of work from the school anyways, and I didn't want Scotty to have to go alone. They lived all the way on the other side of the U.S. in Seattle.

We didn't get to sit together though. We bought our tickets on the day of and were almost the last ones on the plane, so we picked a seat next to a couple of strangers. Man was I excited to get to travel by air finally; before that I had never had any reason to.

I'll never forget the feeling of taking off; it was such a rush when you felt the plane go from touching ground to being in the air so quickly. And the turbulence was so satisfyingly terrifying! The flight itself was about six hours long, so I bought two packs of Dovals just in case and a six-pack of Little Kings to keep myself entertained.

The windows don't open on planes, and everybody was smoking, so I remember breathing in so many different kinds of tobacco. It pissed me off cause I couldn't really enjoy my Doval. Anyways, we landed in Seattle. We touched ground so hard, I was sure we must've crashed, but that was just my naive misunderstanding of how planes work.

I've got to be honest, the *true* reason I was so willing to go to WA with Scotty was because of the most recently accused Seattle-stationed serial killer, Ted Bundy. I was so intrigued with the story. At this time he had just recently been caught in Florida from escaping the Colorado jail in '77, for murdering multiple college women in their 20s.

I wanted to be in the same city, walk the same streets, think the same thoughts where he acquired the inspiration to kidnap all those girls. He was just an intelligent, handsome, curious guy. I wondered if he had a bad childhood like me. *What was the root of his doings?* I wished there was a way to find out. I guess my real confusion streamed from not understanding why people were so upset.

I mean, there are a lot of fucked-up things in the world, and Ted has just found some problems that have a solution, *for him anyway,* but a lot of problems don't. So I think people should just leave him alone and let him make his contribution to the world as he sees fit. Him and I have a lot in common—just trying to help others—they just don't see it yet. Soon though.

Anyway, Seattle was an awesome place. Kind of reminded me of Philly, except five times the size, less homeless people, and a lot more clean. I thought it would've rained a lot, cause that's what you hear about, but it only sprinkled two of the five days we were there, so that was nice. Ya know I've never been a huge fan of the rain. Luckily Steven waited to host his bachelor party until we got there, so that's how we spent our first night there, which was just exhausting after traveling all day. But we still had fun.

We went to some speakeasy called the Blue Moon Tavern and there were some very interesting ladies downstairs. That was my first time encountering strippers, and it was interesting to say the least. What happens in Seattle stays in Seattle. Two days later was the wedding where they had it at the iconic Smith Tower. I guess it's a pretty popular place to host weddings. It was held on the 35th floor and you could see all of Seattle from the 360 degree mesmerizing view. Plus there were minimal people there so I didn't have to socialize as much as I thought I was going to have to.

I met this girl there who was the bridesmaid of the woman Steven married. Her name was River, and she is probably the sexiest woman I've ever met. She had a sun-kissed complexion, with freckles all over her face, probably from spending so much time in the sun. Medium, frizzy, brown hair sat neatly on top of her piercing shoulder blades.

She caught a bus from southern California to make it to the wedding. She was a drifter, I suppose. She didn't have a job or a real home, she just hopped from one place to another with only the clothes on her back and the will of Mother Nature on her side. To be honest with you, I don't remember much about the wedding because I couldn't take my eyes off of Riv once I saw her.

That night at the reception, I approached her and she told me her life story. Her father died when she was young, and her mother was emotionally demeaning towards her, so she left home at 18 and never came back. She hitchhiked from Minnesota along the border to Seattle, which is where she met Steven's wife, Amy. I guess she stayed with her for a few years while Amy was studying in University, and left on good terms with her, with a promise that one day they would reconnect. River hitchhiked down the coast of California until she settled down in San Diego, making a home for herself in the upstairs' corners of a nightbar for free rent, as long as she served drinks there for a low wage.

River had experienced more in life than I had at the time, and I fantasized with her and the adventure of her life. Her style consisted of flare pants and button-up shirts. Sometimes she wore flowy skirts which is what I really liked seeing her in. She didn't believe that showering was a priority.

She said that, "Rain is the most natural shower of all, and the only shower I am destined to have," and I loved that about her. She never even smelled bad; she didn't smell like anything truthfully. I referred to her as a tumbleweed blowing in the wind because she had no plans as to what she was doing or where she was going next. She was as spontaneous and as un-organized as blowing tumbleweed. It only took that one night for me to start falling for her.

There was so much to love about her that I had to attempt a relationship with her. She accepted my invitation to travel back to Delaware with me and experience life with me for as far as the wind took her.

So, I bought her a ticket the next day and held her hand as she sat through her first airplane takeoff, as I acted like I had travelled by plane thousands of times before, while we sipped cheap beer and talked the whole way back. I smoked my last cigarette before getting on the plane, and they didn't sell my kind, so I suffered the whole way back. Good thing I had Riv to talk to for six hours or I probably would've died from nicotine withdrawal.

When we got back, it was obvious that I couldn't just bring a stranger to live in Dawn's house with us. She was already doing me a huge favor—I couldn't ask for more. So River and I immediately started looking for an apartment and found a place within about a week. It was a little further than I wanted but it worked. The place was called Brooksdale and it was about six miles or so from the cemetery, so I actually had to start driving again.

The apartment was a two-bedroom, two-bath area with a cute little balcony (we were on the third floor) which was convenient for my excessive smoking habit. I've always smoked indoors, but Riv always bickered at me for the smell because she was a non-smoker, so I tried to please her by only exhaling outdoors. Dawn had found River a job as a waitress with her, so that was helpful with bills and such. We got along pretty well for two people who moved in together after such little time knowing one another. I was pleasantly surprised, for it was quite nice having someone to keep me company every night. I felt like we had a lot in common.

Looking back on October 11th, 1970 when I first toured my new home on Farghue Lane, I remember being so intrigued by Bettie's style.

The flower-printed sofa, the tiny kitchen covered in cow decorations, the master bedroom that looked like an 80-year old woman's quarters. The bathroom was covered in this nasty, discolored white, peeling wallpaper with pine cones all over it. The bathroom needed work; really bad, honestly. The toilet bowl was stained so badly, you couldn't even tell if it had been flushed yet or not, and pretty much all of the cabinet doors were hanging by a thread.

The only thing that caught my eye in that lavatory was the wood-crafted, triple-tier jewelry box with the initials B.L.M. engraved into the top. There was a keyhole but I think that was just decoration because I was able to get into it no problem. Her parents must have given her that when she was young, perhaps. I didn't really know the full story of it, but that's what I went with. I know that she kept her name when she married Walter, so there's a chance that she got it after that as well, but who cares. All I cared about was what was *inside* this beautiful wooden box. Most of it was sterling silver, a lot of gaudy earrings, and bracelets and such. There were a couple gold rings in there that I believe may have been artificial.

There was a tiny, black, velvet box in the bottom right corner of the third drawer. I opened it with ease, and inside was the most beautiful wedding ring I had ever seen. It was gold— 10 karat, maybe 12 karat: I'm not sure—with one sole diamond resting in it's set, surrounded by intricately designed tiny diamonds set in between the gold.

As soon as I saw it, I immediately placed it back in its box and I kissed the top of it and I thanked Bettie under my breath. Something about that ring gave me hope that I would find a need for it one day.

Thanksgiving, 1980

For a free spirit who mostly only eats what nature provided for her, I never would've expected River really knew how to cook, but man was I wrong. Our first Thanksgiving together in '79, she cooked dinner for Scotty, his wife Sabrina, Dawn, and myself and it was nice but it wasn't anything special because we were still getting adjusted to our new life in a new house. Mainly the dinner consisted of cheesy noodles and beer.

Our second Thanksgiving together was one for the books. She went all out that year, and prepared a turkey the size of a large dog; buttery, homemade mashed potatoes, boxed stuffing (which is better than homemade stuffing honestly), apple, peanut butter, and pecan pies—basically everything you could think of and it was all amazing.

We played cards and drank hot chocolate and told stories from our past 'til late at night and then set up the Christmas tree when midnight came around. Earlier that day we had went and picked out the fullest tree in the lot, cause that's what River wanted.

She picked out her favorite and we strapped it in the back of my pickup and headed to the local store to find some decorations for it, since neither of us had any of our own. It was my first time putting a tree up ever in my adult life; I've just never been much for decorating I guess.

Anyway, I knew a few months prior that I loved that girl. I was going to marry her. I just wanted to wait for the right time to ask her, and that night it felt right. After we finished with the tree I pulled Scotty aside to tell him what I was about to do, just to make sure he agreed and I wasn't being some crazy person. He smiled and put his hand on my shoulder and told me it was the *perfect time,* so I went for it.

I walked over and took her hand, knelt down on one knee and asked her to spend the rest of her life with me. I wish you could have seen the look on her face when she said yes. My god that ring looked amazing on her. Bettie would be so proud. I think she would've wanted River to have that ring. For once I finally felt like I had a family that year, but we all know nothing lasts forever.

River and I tried for six or seven months straight to get pregnant. It was always a hard topic for her to discuss, because after a few doctor's appointments, we were told that it was her who had trouble in that department. I always knew it secretly—there was no way I could be sterile.

She felt like it was her fault though, and we were told that the chances of one of her eggs being fertilized was 1:100. She knew it was never going to happen, but that didn't stop her from trying. She wasn't gonna give up until she got lucky with that one special egg.

Almost every time we had sex, she would sit in the corner for a couple hours mixing her urine and other miscellaneous liquids together like she was in a scientific laboratory. I never saw the point, really. I mean I feel like I would feel a baby inside of me. I don't need some 10-dollar kit to prove it. Whatever made her happy though...

The trash in her bathroom was always full of tests, until one day she lost hope I guess. She started testing once a month only, and all came out negative still. I want to say I didn't really care looking back; ya know as long as I had her then I would be fine.

But, that's not true. I wanted kids. I wanted someone to raise as my own and be a father figure for my child and give them what I never had. Eventually I stopped flipping the tests over in the trash can to see what the result was, because I already knew.

TUESDAY, MAY 12TH, 1981

We were only a couple months out from our wedding date. We were so happy and in love, ready to start our life together and start a family. So we woke up that morning and decided *why wait?* So we called up Scotty and Dawn and we got it rolling. We had decided that we were going to have our ceremony in the beautiful field behind my flower shop. There was no sense in spending a bunch of money for something big since we didn't really have anyone to invite. We just wanted something simple and quick. So they went on a search for a person who could marry us, and on their search of talking to people it just so happened that Ms. Ingrid Robbins was licensed and she agreed to do it for us for free, so that was super convenient. And we had already went to the city hall and done all the paperwork that we needed to take care of. Next was just to do it. So Dawn took Riv to some local vintage consignment shop to find a dress and then the five of us went behind Lynn's and we tied the knot! She looked so incredibly beautiful.

The dress was this cream-colored, lace, high-necked dress with a train the size of a football field in the back. It looked like it was made back in the '50s or something. Dawn had done her hair in some pinned-up braid thing. As for me, I just wore some gray-colored tux with a bow-tie that Scott had let me borrow.

While I was changing into my outfit before the ceremony, Ms. Ingrid came to give me her congratulations. She walked up behind me sliding her hand down the front of my pants, telling me this was our last chance to feel one another. She had always wanted me for some reason; I never really understood it, nor was I ever interested in having an older woman before. But this time it was different. I felt like it was my last chance to be with someone else, cause I was about to commit to forever with Riv. I turned my head slightly to the left so I could get a glimpse of her face to confirm my desires, and then I grabbed her by the waist and swung her around to be in front of me. Nose to nose we started devouring each other's faces. I still don't think I've had a sexier makeout session to this day. I cupped my hands under her tight buttcheeks and lifted her up as she wrapped her legs around my waist, exposing her naked underside. I used one of my arms to hold her and my other to remove my pants. Immediately my hard penis was pointed straight up between her cheeks. I started to move back and forth just so I could tease myself before sticking my throbbing penis inside her, but she was already moaning, which led me to think that maybe she liked it up the ass... I had never had that experience before. I loosened my arm and as she landed on the ground I quickly turned her back around and forced her over to the chair, bending her over. Sucking on her neck, I forced myself inside her. She kept screaming sounds of joy so I didn't stop. I took her by the waist and just fucked her until she couldn't take it anymore.

They aren't lying when they say older women know what they're doing. She knew what she wanted. She knew how to do it. She was sure of herself. It was tantalizing. It made me sad that it took me 'til my wedding day to be able to embrace her, but I certainly do not regret it; that was the best sex I've ever had. We finished, got dressed, and walked out of the room like nothing happened and we went to get me married. It was a nice and simple half hour and we were officially husband and wife. Afterwards we went to Scott's bar. He had arranged for food from an Italian restaurant to be catered there for us and whatever other locals decided to celebrate our marriage with us and we just ate and drank and danced all night. I couldn't have imagined it any other way.

THANKSGIVING, 1981

Earlier that morning before Riv and I started preparing food I went to use her bathroom because mine was out of toilet paper and it was time for my morning shit. I'm sitting there, doing my daily crossword and I glanced down at the trash can and saw the biggest mess I had ever seen. It was disgusting. Bloody rags, used tissues, THREE empty toothpaste containers. She hadn't taken out her trash in the time it took her to

use three entire tubes of dental paste! Enough was enough—
I decided to take it out for her because clearly she wasn't going
to do it. I flushed my excessive amount of toilet paper down
the toilet and started hauling the trash can out when I heard
Riv call out to me, "Graham! I need help with some things!"

She was frantically running around the house trying to
prepare for the festivities that night, and when she saw me
holding the trash she became even more stressed out. I guess
I "wasn't doing what I was supposed to be doing" and I needed
to "get back to the task at hand." "I'll take that out before dinner tonight. Don't worry about that right now," she said. I did
as told and set it back in the bathroom. Nasty. My task at
hand was to go to the car to get the centerpiece for the table.
When I saw some daisies in a big yellow vase in the backseat
of the car, I almost passed out.

Our Thanksgiving centerpiece couldn't possibly be daisies.
"Was she pranking me? She knew I despised those putrid
things...she must be setting me up?" I thought. I didn't know
how to react. "Do I bring them in? Do I dispose of them and
act like nothing was in the car?" Hope led me to believe everything would be okay so I carried them into the house with a
smile on my face and placed them in the center of the table as
I heard her exclaim, "Oh! They're just the perfect color for
Thanksgiving! I'm so happy that the neighbors down the
street decided to go out of town last minute and gave them to
us!" She wanted me to trim the stems. Why? Why did she
have to do that? Why did she have to destroy what could have
been a perfect evening? I had told her the stories about Paul.
She knew about the flowers and what they did to me.

I tried not to let it ruin my evening. I tried so hard to for-

get about it—not to look over at them. I could *smell* them…
My mind wouldn't stop running. I was afraid for anyone to
leave. That was the main reason I tried having them stay for as
long as I possibly could. But eventually they had to go home
and in that moment I went directly to my room and locked the
door. I had to be alone.

I was scared of myself. I was just trying to think about my
Mama at that point. I needed her to talk some good thoughts
into my head; I needed her to be there for me, but she wasn't.
I remember when she used to say to me "…everything will be
okay because tomorrow is a new day. I love you Graham
Embry Soyle, and I always will…"

I can remember one time when I was about 10 or so and I
started having these horrid dreams every night, not just
nightmares. Like this shit was real. I sometimes couldn't tell
my dreams from reality and for a 10-year-old that's pretty
scary.

Anyway, one specific night I had a dream that when my
Mama had me she went into a rage and murdered me, like she
started stabbing me rapidly over and over and over with a
screwdriver. Obviously I woke up screaming and crying and
she rushed into my bedroom and just laid down and held me
tight, telling me everything was going to be okay and that she
would always be there for me no matter what. Well, Mama,
everything isn't okay and I need you now, and you aren't here
for me. So what now?

Graham Embry Soyle
12/12/06

Friday, November 27th, 1981

The night after Thanksgiving and I was still recovering from the great disappointment that River put me through the night before. I hadn't talked to her since I locked myself in my room. I had snuck out earlier than I normally do for work so that I wouldn't have to face her. I just needed some time alone. I headed to the cemetery and had a long conversation in my head about how to talk to River.

How to apologize. I knew that she wasn't trying to hurt me so I couldn't hold it against her. I just wanted things to be good again. And that was huge for me! I had never given anyone a second chance before her, and I never have since. So after my walk to work, I gave her a call and asked if she wanted to meet me there for lunch. She agreed. Meanwhile I started my normal daily chores; mowing, cleaning up, watering the plants, and, the last thing I always did, digging graves. I remember there was only one for that day so I finished it around the time River showed up. She had actually kind of spooked me. I guess I had lost track of time when she came up behind me and said my name. So we stood there and talked. I had it all planned out:

"Sorry I had to leave early this morning, I just needed to clear my head," I started, knowing it wasn't going to go anywhere.

"Eh, it was nice to get to sleep in," she said as if it were a complete lie.

"Well I just wanted to apologize for last night. I kind of lost myself a little." I wasn't sorry.

"Graham, you don't need to apologize." She lied about

that, too, but who could blame her.

And then we hugged. A beautiful long, tight, loving hug. It was as if nothing had happened, as if she never did anything wrong.

But she couldn't leave the conversation like that... She just had to open her mouth again... her daisy-picking, daisy-supporting, daisy-loving personality just had to reveal itself again and she opened her mouth once more.

"I've been feeling strange lately. We just want different things, I think. I'm ready for a family, I'm ready to settle down. You're so caught up with this damn graveyard! You're always here. I don't want to be the one to hold you back from what you want... and I think we both know that there are things you need to work out with yourself. It's not fair for you, and I want you to be happy because I love you. I want the best for you, and the best for myself. I've been trying to find the right time to tell you something, and I'm not sure how you're going to take..."

Before she could even finish, my eyes quickly went from peacefully shut to painfully open when I not only heard those words come from her mouth but also saw that she had those fucking daisies tucked in her back pocket. I looked at her with rage in my eyes and I literally saw my good-for-nothing father's face in place of hers! It was just sitting there, looking at me, asking me for forgiveness. At that point, my arms went from holding her tight to forcefully shoving her forward. And no, I hadn't forgotten that I had just dug a six-foot grave directly behind her. But she deserved to be in there and suffer more than the poor old man I had originally dug it out for. She was a selfish bitch for breaking my heart and betraying my mother with those god-forsaken flowers and I wanted her to pay.

So I started throwing the loose dirt on top of her face as she stood up screaming, begging me to stop. It was oddly satisfying watching a 5'2" woman trying to get out of a 6'0" deep hole. I had never buried someone alive before, and as much as I enjoyed listening to her cry for help, I couldn't have anyone hearing her, so I grabbed my shovel and smacked her over the head with it as hard as I could, watching her fall over and her scalp start to bleed. I just watched her for a second, her eyes wide open, but not quite conscious.

Her neck slightly twitching. I could see her arm try to reach up, and her mouth try to open to tell me to stop, but she didn't have the strength. I would like to say she fell down gracefully, but she didn't. She just fell, and her eyes just stared back at me, almost lifelessly. It wasn't until I saw the dirt fall into her bleach-white eyes that I knew she was done for. And for a split second I almost felt bad, because I did love her. I just couldn't hold back my anger towards her. So I moved on and continued watching her body disappear underneath the earth as I continued tossing dirt on top of her. Vern must have been eavesdropping on our conversation because he appeared next to me with a shovel and started tossing dirt into the grave as well. I'm not sure he even realized what he was assisting me with? But, what he didn't know couldn't hurt him I guess.

Anyways, I loved it. Can you imagine being responsible for someone who dies? It's just kind of amazing. I mean really, it's going to happen anyway, but just think of being the person in control of it happening... it's insane. Literal insanity. You kind of feel like God. You control it. You control *them*. They weren't supposed to die, but then you made it happen. With your own two hands. *You.* That's right. *You.* I don't blame you for thinking about it, cause I know you are. You can't *not*. I know you want to know how it feels, and I can try and try and try to explain it to you but you will never understand until you experience it. It's like no feeling you have ever felt. Nothing you could ever compare to anything in this world. It's euphoric.

The only issue was that the 8 x 3 x 6 foot deep grave I dug was meant for Earl Sappano, and it was spaced exactly six feet apart from the gravesites to the left and to the right, and it was also in my burial spreadsheets as being Earl Sappano's resting place and only his resting place.

So I ended up putting just enough dirt over River to just cover her body, then I ended up throwing good ol' Earl in there in his casket on top of River, so... technically my spreadsheets never lied. He is in there. He just happens to have a friend staying with him for life. It felt kind of weird, but it also felt kind of right. Earl's burial wasn't an open ceremony. Ya know everybody came later and had a service and shit but they didn't see him in the ground, so I knew no one would ever find Riv in there.

But I was also worried about people noticing her being gone. Obviously people were going to know. Her work, our friends. "How am I going to fake that? Did I just fuck this up?" I remember thinking. I had to think on my feet and come up with a good plan.

I always did the best brainstorming in the shower, and so I went into River's old bathroom because her showerhead had a higher intensity and I heated it up to a warm temperature.

Not cold, not lukewarm, and definitely not scorching hot how she liked it, but just the right warm temperature. I got really upset in the shower because I kept looking at all of her shampoo bottles and soaps, and it made me miss her. I needed to get rid of it all.

I started tossing the bottles into the trash can beside the toilet, and of course I missed because she never took the trash out and it was spewing over the top so now there was just a giant pile of shit on the floor. I kicked the can out of rage and knocked the entire thing over, creating an even larger disaster for me to clean later. I didn't even pay much attention to it because I was trying to rinse off, until I saw an object in my peripheral vision through a crack in the shower curtain. I staggered out of the shower, chillingly wet, grasping onto the towel rack to regain my balance, and I slipped on the tile, falling to the ground, coming face to face with the mess. A pregnancy test.

It looked different than all the other ones I had seen in the wastebasket. All I could see was a dark colored ring at the bottom of a test tube. Dark reddish brown in color, a perfect circle... That ring continues to haunt me in my nightmares and my dreams and in my everyday life. A pregnancy test. That must have been what River wanted to tell me before I ended her life... her life and my baby's life. How did I ever forgive myself for that? I'll tell you how...when I get to that point. I don't care that I killed River. That bitch deserved to die for what she did. She did it to herself. But, my poor child didn't know any better. Fuck, it wasn't even a fetus yet; it was just a little sperm cell, but it was my sperm cell. She did this to my child. She killed it with her own actions and rebellious attitude towards me. If your spirit is out there, my beloved child that never was, know that I never meant to hurt you. I only meant to hurt her and you suffered because of it, and I am sorry.

Have you ever thought about what it would feel like to have a noose around your neck?

Graham Embry Soyle
12/25/06

Valentines Day, 1974

A pretty popular time of the year for my shop; the biggest money maker for me. Guys coming in and out all day trying to have flowers delivered to their ladies. Made me sick. But, it kept the business running. I would also stock up on cards and chocolates for the ones who wanted to go all out. You would think that everyone would want either red or pink roses, but nope. There were always a couple of those weirdos who wanted to try and be different. And of course the one guy, *Roy Barker,* who came in asking for Daisies. Fuckin' daisies. Like this was a day of love... the man should have been buying his woman some beautiful smelling roses or peonies... but *clearly* Roy Barker wasn't a romantic guy and I had to take even more time out of my day to save this poor girl from the piece of shit who was buying her daisies instead of a dozen gorgeous roses.

When you fill out the slip of where you want the flowers delivered to (which in that specific case was the girlfriend's work
office), you also have to put down a home address.

So, I knew exactly where I had to go. The young lady didn't
deserve to receive something so vile on Valentine's Day, so I
snatched some white roses from Alfred Hegwein's grave and
delivered those to Roy's girlfriend instead. She opened the
door with the biggest smile on her face and hearts in her eyes
when she saw that bouquet... And people say I'm not nice...
Hah! What a joke! I'm fucking Cupid! I'm a nice-ass mother-
fucker who makes miracles happen... to people who deserve
miracles of course.

Those who don't get the mean side of Graham. Speaking of
people who deserve brutality, I headed straight to Mr. Barker's
home address. He lived in a higher-up neighborhood, one I
had never even driven through. Some gated community or
something. Of course there was the chance that he wasn't
going to be there, but I needed to check anyway. And there sat
a Black Cadillac in the driveway. Rich bitch. I had it planned
out: a quick knife to the top of the spinal cord would put him
right on his face. So I had walked up to the door and he answered with a confused look on his face as to why the guy he
had just bought flowers from was at his front door and not the
person that I was supposed to be delivering them to. Ha. I
don't even think that I said anything. I just went for it, and I
got 'em on the first stab. He instantly became paralyzed and
fell over onto the floor, shaking as if I had stunned him with a
tasegun. It was like hitting a dart on bullseye.

It felt great! At first I figured I would just throw him in the
back of my truck and take him to the cemetery to get rid of

him like the rest of the evidence, but then I thought, I'm too proud of this one. I wanted a constant reminder of the great work I had accomplished. So I brought him with me and this time I buried the guy right next to my office, where I could see him every day. When I finished I placed a nice big pot over top of him and filled it with some seeds to grow peppers. This was going to be the start of my new garden! And Mr. Barker was going to be the unknown fertilizer for the plants.

DECEMBER, 1981

Went as I suspected. It only took a couple days for people to start realizing Riv wasn't around. And obviously I had to go along with it. First, Dawn approached me asking why she hadn't shown up for her shifts the last couple of days. I told her that we had gotten into an argument and she was going away for a couple days to cool off and that I hadn't seen her since. I immediately regretted it because I knew there was no way to follow up with that story once the police were to get involved. Luckily she also didn't have any family, at least none that I was aware she spoke with anyway. So I had that going for me.

There wasn't really anyone who would report her as missing besides myself, her work, or Scotty. And I had already told them my side of the story so they didn't really have a reason to doubt my word.

For all they knew she left town and just didn't return. Luckily that's exactly what happened: no one ever questioned me after that. No one noticed that she had fallen off the face of the earth, literally. Well pushed, but you get it. So I just went on with my boring life after that. Had the apartment to myself with no interest in getting a roommate, even if it was out of my price range. I was back to only having two people in my life that I bothered to associate with voluntarily. And I was basically back to my normal daily routine again. Interesting to compare my life in the '80s to what it was back in '67 when I was new to Meerdin.

7:00 AM: *Wake up and brush my nicotine-stained teeth with baking soda.* It was always cheaper than paste and ya know what Mama said about making 'em sparkle. I picked up flossing a little bit, just because I loved the feeling of the string in between my gums.

7:30 AM: *Drive to Murphy Creek to open the gate and take notes of the flowers I saw there that were still fresh that I knew I could come back for.*

8:00 AM: *Walk over to Lynn's Petals.* Yeh, I was 35 years old and I was the proud business owner of a local flower shop and the keeper and owner of an old grave-yard. Was a pretty good job and made enough to cover my bills each month.

8:10 AM: *Prepare the delivery orders for that day and help David open up.* Typically I had 10 or 15 deliveries to make in a day and I would try to knock that out while I left David (my new hire, ever since Blake left the picture) to run the store. So my business was a unique one. Just to remind you, customers thought I got all my flowers from a merchant or a field that I grew my-self. Nobody knew I ripped them off of people's graves, and I never told anybody. The shop was small and obviously didn't carry a surplus of plants like your typical place. I had a slim selection for walk-ins to pick from; your basic shit really... roses, carnations, lilies. If someone wanted something other than that, they had to put in a special request and place a delivery. I did not offer same-day delivery due to my having to go and steal them.

However, I offered next day, or two-day delivery, and then I would decide what the person got based on the availability of the requested flower. That's why I went to the graveyard every morning before opening the store to take notes of what flowers were available to customers.

9:30 AM: *Set forth on my delivering journey for the day.* I stopped meeting Ingrid everyday after I quit my paper-boy job, but after running into her at the hardware store that one day, I began meeting her around the same time for tea like we used to. I only went once or twice a week though. She was getting pretty old at that point and it became more difficult for her to hold conversations and do normal everyday things. She's probably dead now, and it kills me to think that I missed saying goodbye to her. On Mondays and Wednesdays I met her around this time, but the rest of the week, I just went on with my deliveries. I took my truck with me on the delivery route, which was strange for me cause I was so used to walking.

10:00 AM: *Stop at Lloyd's Locals,* where I bought two packs of Dovals and a Hershey bar. What can I say? I mean, over the years I started smoking more and eating worse... whatever.

1:00–3:00 PM: *Finish my deliveries for the day.* Depending on how many deliveries I had and how many of those deliveries needed "special attention" (which was at least once every two weeks, if not more), I would typically finish dropping off all the flowers by 3:00 PM.

3:15 PM: *Return to the shop and get the next day delivery information from David.* Usually, if it was slow enough, I would send that kid home and cover him until we closed at six, mainly because I never had anything better to do. I liked being alone anyway so I had privacy to sort out my matters. But, occasionally I enjoyed his company and just stayed with him. Poor kid. He had no fucking clue what he was involved in. Good little worker though. I wonder where he's at now? Oh yeah. Dead.

5:30 PM: *Walk over to the bar next door, and take my Scotch shot* which still happened to be Scott's believe it or not. We were like brothers at this point, but wasn't working as much because he was trying to spend all of his time with his wife, Sabrina. Nice girl. Not my type at all, but a nice girl. He just never had enough time for me anymore—he put all of his energy into her.

6:00 PM: *Wrap up some final things and lock the doors to the flower shop.* Everyday before I left, I always looked at the store for a minute and smiled because I was so proud of myself for owning my own business. I couldn't believe it actually. I miss it. I miss the feeling of having power.

6:15 PM: *Head back to the graveyard to lock the gate and go flower shopping.* I had a good system set up and it rarely failed. I knew which flowers were fresh enough to sell, and I kept track of what I had and where they were laying, so at the end of the day, I just walked to the different plots and snatched what I needed. I used to think it was fucked up, but I got over it.

There was this one guy, Spencer Buchanan, that gave me trouble a while back. He wanted to know why every time he came to visit his wife at the graveyard, her flowers had been removed. I tried to explain to him that they were rotting and were attracting bugs. That shut his mouth for a little while, but not enough to where I felt safe. Mr. Buchanan was a threat to me and my nice system, so I struck him with a club one day in the yard. Needless to say, I took care of him. I buried him two feet away from his wife out of respect. You're welcome, Sir.

7:00 PM: *Drop the flowers off at Lynn's Petals.*

7:30 PM: *Come home to my empty apartment.* I had a two bedroom, two bathroom. I wasn't planning on River acting out and ruining my life, so I planned on staying in that house for a while. She used to always cook, too. I would come home every day and there would be dinner at the table. After she wasn't there anymore, I had to start cooking for myself again, and it was awful. I certainly wasn't gonna go back to eating like a poor man just because I didn't have a wife to prepare it. I ended up buying some cookbooks and nailing a few recipes down. Option 1: grilled chicken breast, cut-up red potatoes seasoned with salt and pepper, and corn on the cob. Option 2: Flank steak with cinnamon-glazed carrots and cheesy noodles. Option 3: A full breakfast with dippin' eggs, chocolate-chip pancakes, shredded potatoes and cheese, crispy bacon, and buttery biscuits. On the NON-cooking side, my options were either 4: Canned soup or 5: Go out to eat with Scotty or by myself.

8:00 PM: *Pick a food option and run with it.* I usually picked Option 1, 4, or 5. Steak and breakfast happened once or twice a week, maybe. It just took so much energy out of me after a long day's work. Sometimes I just didn't feel up to it.

8:30 PM: *Cigarette break.* I stopped smoking on the balcony after River was no longer present and I started going outside and taking walks again. These after-dinner-smoke walks were my times to reflect on the day and on my life as a whole. I was so content with my life at the time. Ya know I was living the highest life I could possibly live, and I loved every second of it. For once, I was truly happy. I was happy with being alone and being secretive and being independent.

9:00 PM: *Pop the top off of six beers.* Yes, six beers at the same time. I liked to go to bed with a slight buzz making my head spin, so I typically just chugged all six as quick as I could. Once I started my nightly six-pack ritual, it was hard to fall asleep without the slight buzz. So, I kept doing it... every night... until November 15th, 1984, of course. Damn what I would do for a Little Kings right now. Sure, sometimes a few bottles may sneak their way in here every so often, but they were never Little Kings. It was always some home-made shit that didn't even take the edge off.

9:30 PM: *Bedtime.* I went to bed nice and easy, ready to wake up the next morning and repeat my day.

Graham Embry Soyle
01/06/07

TOBACCO

Relaxation, Healing, and Peace

Monday, July 25th, 1983

I **was walking alongside the shallow spaced,** dirt sidewalk for what seemed like hours and hours. I couldn't believe Scotty tried to take me out of his life. That wasn't the answer; that wasn't going to solve his problems. I mean, seriously. Did he not think I would find my way back to Meerdin? It's not like he dropped me off at the top of Mount Everest. After reading miles and miles of road signs, I figured out I was in Burlington, West Virginia. I remember sticking my left thumb out as far as my arm could reach. I felt like a roamer... I felt like I was free of everything... I felt at peace almost. I felt like maybe how Riv felt back in her earlier days and I started feeling sad thinking about Riv and the memories we had made and then I remembered how she destroyed those memories.

My thumb was out for approximately four minutes when I heard a loud engine slowing down beside me. I opened my eyes and came out of my imaginative flashback trance and saw the most beat up, forest-green colored pick-up truck I had ever seen in my life. Two of the tires were slowly, but surely deflating. The paint was peeling off in more than five locations, the left side mirror was non-existent, as well as the majority of the door handles.

The noise that was escaping this vehicle resembled a cry for help from a tiny, shrieking donkey and occurred in spurts every 45 seconds or so. Everything about this truck told me not to get in it. So what did I do? I walked up, waited for the woman inside to open the passenger door from the inside because my handle was missing, and I hopped in next to her. Never got her name actually. I wasn't in there long enough to find out.

I had never hitchhiked before this moment. It was always just an idea that I knew of from stories or films. I never knew if people actually hitchhiked or not, but there I was, riding shotgun next to a total stranger in a dying pick-up truck. I mean, honestly, everything about the concept is peculiar. Why a thumb? Why are you supposed to stick your thumb out? What kind of signal is that? And then just randomly jumping in the first car that stops, not knowing who it is, or where they are going... so bizarre. Immediately upon my ass making contact with the torn fabric seat, the mysterious woman took off and said, "Can you hand me a cold one? They're in the cooler in the back. Help yourself to one, too, but only one please. Those have to last me until I get to Dover." She was so intoxicated already though, that the whole statement she said actually blurred together as one giant mumble and sounded something like, "Cuun ya hunmeh colon...in back...you shave one, too, but ONLY ONE boy ha ha ha, lasted me alls theway til Dov ha ha ha."

Needless to say, I was shocked and horrified not only because she was driving a motorized vehicle and she asked me for an alcoholic beverage, but because there were already two empty bottles in the cupholders and three empty bottles on the floor of the car!

This woman was on her way to Dover, which was perfect for me. Theoretically, I could've made it all the way back home with this drunk woman and possibly had a good time doing it. I definitely considered it, but decided I wanted to return to my life in Meerdin alive. If I stayed with drunkie, I probably would've been uncovered from a ditch a few days later on the side of the highway. So, as usual, I thought I was making a good choice... but it turned out to be the wrong choice. I had a better chance of survival with the intoxicated nut than I did with my next designated driver, but I'll get into that in a minute.

Something came over me and I shouted, "PULL OVER!" She obeyed and dropped me next to this magnificent concrete overpass. I decided I would keep moving forward on foot (at least until I saw another car). I enjoyed walking on the side of an isolated highway. It was peaceful and I felt safe enough to where I stopped worrying about everything I had going on in life and I just appreciated the crisp morning air. I had been walking now for probably five-and-a-half hours after the drunken lady left me by the overpass... so about a full 14 hours since Scotty had left me for dead.

I remember coming across a gigantic field of tobacco plants, right off the side of the highway. It was unusual to say the least. I mean, I always saw wheat and corn fields off the highway, but I had never seen a tobacco farm in person until that very day. It was so quiet and peaceful, I decided to have a stroll through the perfectly-plowed rows of tobacco. I know nothing about farming, so I had no idea if the leaves were ready or not, but I ended up plucking a few off of one meaty looking plant. Not like I knew how the fuck to extract tobacco from the leaves... I don't know what I was thinking really, but it was a memory that obviously played some kind of role in my ever-depressing life because I am repeating the story to you now. Anyways, I sat amongst the unborn cigarettes for a couple of hours, just resting. I managed to finish off the last of my Dovals and was starting to get anxious. That's when I decided to come back to the side of the road in hopes of joining a driver for a wonderful journey back home so I could take care of Scotty.

When I returned to the bank of the concrete, there was already a car stopped in the dirt. A tiny, compact, four-door Ford in good condition with a 50-something-year-old man driving it. Looked good to me! Strangely, he seemed to have been sitting there as if he were waiting for me. I mean, c'mon. I didn't even stick my thumb out now that I'm thinking about it. I just opened the passenger door and got in. First of all, he questioned where my bags were (I guess hitchhikers usually have backpacks with them) but I just sort of ignored him and changed the subject.

Fast forward a few hours: Joe (the guy who picked me up by the tobacco) and I were getting along just fine. He seemed like a pretty friendly guy, actually. He was single, no kids, in his early 50s with no real responsibilities. He was a fisherman for a small company, or so he said, and he talked a lot about his trailer house. Was really proud of it or something. Who knows. The best way I can describe him is as a "cool dad" figure. Ya know whenever you sleepover at your friend's house and the friend's dad is cooler than your own dad. Like ya know the friend's dad isn't *actually* cooler than your own dad but he comes off to be because he's trying so hard with snacks and fun activities and shit but in reality the friend's dad probably snorted cocaine off of prostitute's breasts after work. Yeh, that was Joe. Joe the cool dad I never had.

We drove and drove. Just talking about our lives, not a care in the world. He had a little tinge of creepiness to him, but I never even thought about it because his coolness overcame all that. I felt safe enough with him. Safe enough that I agreed to ride with him all the way back to Meerdin when he offered out of kindness.

The two of us were enjoying each other's company so much that we completely missed the sun fade away and the moon appeared. Joe was starting to yawn and doze off at the wheel for a couple seconds at a time, when he saw a sign that he recognized, I guess. He shouted, "Hey! My home is just off this bend here. Do ya mind if we pull off and crash tonight? We can get started fresh and early in the morning. Whaddya say?"

Again, I felt safe with Joe. Safe enough that I agreed to stay in his tiny, white, scary, 8 x 6 foot trailer in the middle of an abandoned farm. Looking back on it, it truly could've been a scene from a horror film: Sheets of fog billowing around the overgrown crops and the dirt road that led directly to the front door of Joe's "home." Inside, he had a little kitchen and a television set and a sleepaway sofa. It was homey; I could see why he was so proud of it. So yeh, we slept side by side on this sofa bed thing and I never felt uncomfortable in any type of way.

Flash forward to the next morning: I woke up to nobody beside me, with a neon green post-it note stuck to my forehead that read, "Sorry kid, last minute work needed this mornin'. Hang tight here and don't worry. We'll get back on the road soon. Make yourself at home. —Joe."

Even if I had a weird feeling about the note, it's not like I could've really done anything about it. I was there alone, in the middle of nowhere in a random city. Joe was my way back to my life and I couldn't just throw that away because the plan changed course. I trusted he would follow through with his promise to take me home, so I stayed at the abandoned farm and just relaxed that day, waiting for him to come home from work. Little did I know, he embarked on a three-day fishing expedition...

Day Number One: That's when I woke up, probably around noon or so and found the note. I pretty much just laid in bed for a while contemplating on whether or not I should stay or go. After making my decision to wait for Joe, I decided to adventure off and wander the farm to see what interesting things I could find. Turned out to be nothing of particular interest to me. I found a couple of random tools tossed in the overgrown fields, some handwoven baskets, tons of dead crops scattered across the land, some beautiful rose bushes in the far right-hand corner of the lot, and other boring things. The most interesting find was a red barn the size of a red suburban home, with a huge rusted lock clasping the doors shut. The lock looked like it hadn't come off in a while, but I remember there being a very strong, foul odor excreting from the cracks. It smelled of dead animals, like perhaps the person who abandoned the farmland left the chickens and cows and things inside the farmhouse, too. Whatever it was, I walked quickly away from it to get that stench out of my nostrils. Fast forward to:

Day Number Two: I woke up early in hopes of seeing Joe had returned, but all I woke up to was silence. I didn't eat the night before because I had never been given permission to eat his food. He seemed like a nice guy though and I felt safe enough there in his trailer so I started rummaging through his "kitchen" cabinets and drawers. I found some crackers, rotten milk, and then a surprisingly fresh orange, which I took the liberty upon scarfing down. I had a feeling that one mouthful of citrus wouldn't be enough to hold me over for the day though. I reached into my pocket and found some cash from when I first checked into the insane asylum. They gave me back all my original belongings when I got released.

I remembered seeing a bicycle leaned up against the side of the trailer the day before, so I hopped on that, determined to bike myself into town for some food and cigarettes. I biked about four miles or so before I started seeing some regular traffic flow. I powered forward another half mile and happened upon the small town of Worrington, Maryland. Apparently, I was right on the corner of Delaware, so Scotty must have dropped me further than I thought. I pulled over at the first little convenience store I saw. I don't remember the name of it, but it reminded me of Lloyd's Locals back home. There was a real friendly old guy behind the counter. He's the one who told me what town I was in and it's proximity to Dover.

He was curious as to why I was there, of course, so I told him my whole story, beginning at the tobacco field and ending with the trailer. I didn't continue with the story because the look on this man's face was concerning. He looked like he had just seen a ghost or something. He muttered, "Joe, huh? You're staying with Joe?" I was surprised because I never told this man his name, but, "yeh," I said. "I'm staying with Joe the fisherman." "You're fucked, young man. You're absolutely fucked," old friendly guy said through his chuckles. He put his elbows on the countertop and leaned in to me and whispered, "Son, I suggest you bike back to Joe's tiny little trailer, park the bike exactly where you found it in the first place, start running back towards town and never look back." He handed me the pack of Dovals and the cold-cut sandwich I was about to purchase and gave them to me "on the house" and told me "Good Luck!" Now, I probably should've done what this man told me to do, but I kinda ignored his warnings.

Honestly, I thought he was bluffing. He didn't know me, I didn't know him. What reason did he have to tell me something like that? I walked down the town's strip of shops, browsed around a few stores, and remembered I left the bike at the convenience store. I started walking back that way so that I could head back towards the trailer. When I made it back to the store, I saw that the blue bicycle with one tire flatter than the other was not where I left it. It was gone. Someone from that dumbass littleass lyingass town stole Joe's bicycle! I remember being panicky and wondering how I was going to explain to him what had happened.

Day Number Three: Joe finally came back, but he didn't have too much to say. He was pretty chatty before so perhaps something happened. I never found out. He got there, told me we were leaving and that's exactly what we did. No questions from me. Those people from town were wrong cause he never even noticed that his bike was gone. Must've been a town rumor they had goin' on. Who knows. He got me back to Meerdin and I went straight to the bar to take care of business.

Thursday, July 28th, 1983

There he was. Typical, predictable Scotty. I walked in like there was nothing out of the ordinary. There were several people in there so when he looked over and saw me, he was forced to react nonchalantly. I smirked and sat down at the bar directly in front of where he was standing behind it. "Scotch, Scotty?" He poured us a double without ever breaking eye contact with me. We threw them back and began talking as if nothing even happened. He betrayed our friendship and that was now my plan, too. I only sipped on a couple beers for the remainder of the time, staying 'til close. I was obviously the last one there besides Scotty, which is when he finally had the nerve to ask me how I made it back. There wasn't any time for catching up. He lost that privilege. I aimlessly jumped over the counter and tackled him into the ground.

I wasn't sure what I wanted to do with him until I was face to face with him; me on top and him looking like a scared little child trembling, telling me *"NO!"* I knew then that I didn't want this to be brutal. I held him down and told him to stop. I told him I felt betrayed and that I was going to kill him, whether it be easy or hard, but that I preferred him to cooperate with me. Crying, he nodded his head and said that he would. Before I left it up to trust, I grabbed a handful of his hair and yanked his head backwards and with the other hand I grabbed a bottle of Scotch and started pouring it down his throat until he began to choke, spitting it back out. I started pouring again. And again. I kept going until he finally let himself swallow it. That's when I let go of his hair, and he knew what was happening.

With his shaking hands he ripped the bottle back from me and started chugging it. Still crying, he stopped for a second to tell me that he was sorry but I didn't care anymore. He continued until the bottle was empty and shortly after, passed out. I watched him laying there. No sign of breathing. No pulse. I was a tad bit sad, but mainly I felt glad that it was over. One less person to care about. I left him there and went home. He was found the next day dead. Apparently he had drugs in his system so I guess that helped get the job done, too, but they deemed it suicide. Easy enough for me.

Graham Embry Soyle
01/06/07

PRIMROSE

FEMININITY

SOMETIME IN 1974

S *ome dumbass named* **Brent Gentry** put in an order for
three daisies to be delivered to his mother-in-law for her
birthday. I think this one pissed me off a little more mainly
because he resembled Paul, so I just wanted to be extra ass-
hole-ish to him.

I had this idea to just kill him with rat poison. I had actually thought of the idea because one night when I was walking
home I saw a needle on the ground that I only assumed someone had used to inject heroin or something. But it intrigued
me so I swiped it and took it home.

Anyway, I went to our local drug store and bought some
rat poison and sucked it up into the needle, carefully stowed it
away, and brought it with me on my little "delivery." So there I

went, wandering up to this guy's door, knocking on it, and waiting patiently. I was excited about this one; it was something new. And also I was just curious about what exactly was going to happen. He opened the door and I asked if I could come in for a minute, which he agreed to and invited me to the living room.

When he turned around to guide me in the direction, I immediately injected him with the poison by jabbing the needle into the side of his neck. He started gasping and holding his neck with his hands because he couldn't breathe, and then he put himself on the floor while he choked. At that point he started to foam at the mouth. His eyes went bloodshot as they started to roll towards the back of his head and then began to have convulsions. It was certainly the most entertaining of the kills I've had. So that was nice; something different. Now I just had to get him to the cemetery. But first, I wanted to have a look around.

It was a small house with only one bedroom so there wasn't much for me to explore. I assumed that the guy was single cause he seemed to be quite the pervert. He had a bunch of playboy magazines and dildos lying around the place. Although I did find a pretty nice gold bracelet lying on a nightstand in his room. Figured I'd go ahead and take that off his hands for 'em. The kitchen was a mess, like he hadn't cleaned it in months. There were literal stacks of dirty dishes and pizza boxes lying everywhere. Build-ups of dirt in every corner you looked at, holes all over the walls, and there were roaches scurrying all around the floors and counters, which was just fucking disgusting. I did Meerdin a favor by getting rid of this scumbag.

WEDNESDAY, JANUARY 25TH, 1989

I was peacefully eating my *so-called-food* for lunch when I overheard two of the guards discussing how the famous Ted Bundy had gotten killed by the electric chair the day before. I guess before he was executed, he admitted to around 30 or so murders of women. I betcha he only confessed so he could be remembered.

I mean really, how many people from prison do you know the names of because they killed one or two or even three people? You don't. You only know of the ones that go on a rampage and kill lots of people. And that's what he did. He made himself a *story*. What a smart bastard he was. And that was the day I decided I was going to do the same thing; I began writing my story. Get ready to remember Graham Embry Soyles, for the rest of your *lives*.

WEDNESDAY, AUGUST 14TH, 1974

I was slaving away at the shop on a Wednesday. I remember it was a Wednesday for some reason. Anyways, I had already made the deliveries for the day and sent Blake home. As a matter of fact I was fixing to close up, I believe. These two bubbly people came in, husband and wife, and they were smiling from ear to ear. They were the happiest set of people I had seen in my whole life, and to this day I've never seen anyone as positive as them. I can't stand people who are that happy, first of all. How can someone possibly be that happy? It's fake. Fake emotions. Real people express happiness, and anger, and irritability, and sadness. So don't walk into my store flaunting off only one fake emotion cause it will piss me off, and you don't wanna see me pissed off. I was minutes away from closing when they walked in, so I was already in a bad mood. It didn't help that they were surrounding me with their happiness. And then, guess what they wanted delivered?! Three daisies, one for each of their children. When those words came out of their mouths, I almost killed them right then and there.

However, I held my anger in. I didn't even have daisies in stock at the graveyard, but I didn't care. They were gonna be getting a special delivery the next day. I gave them the paperwork to fill out and watched them sign their names "William Simone" and "Alexandria Simone," knowing that that was probably the last time they would ever sign their names. I was a cash-only business, because I didn't want any of my victims getting traced back to my shop with a check or something. That was too risky. I collected money before I made deliveries. That way I still received payment for those customers who never got the chance to receive their flowers. However, with this special couple, I decided I would kill them for free. I told them, "Sorry for the trouble, the delivery is on me. See you tomorrow."

So, "tomorrow" came. It was about 1:15 PM and all of my regular deliveries were finished for the day. The Simones were my only delivery that required special attention, so I could really put all of my energy into it. I showed up to their front door, empty-handed, and knocked to the tune of "Shave and a Haircut." Alexandria opened the door up with that wide grin on her face, and immediately looked worried because I wasn't bearing any daisies. I asked if she would allow me inside and she said, "Uh-h I don't know if that is the best i-idea... my husband isn't home. He is at work-k."... "Fuck! I had to wait to kill William, too! He was so excited about these fucking daisies. He deserves to suffer just as much as his happy little wife," I remember thinking. I couldn't risk her closing the door in my face, so I grabbed her head and beat it against the door hinge. Blood started spewing from her hairline, but it wasn't enough. She easily could've escaped.

So, I smashed her head down two more times, hitting the same mark each time. The look of life flushed from her eyes. She looked like she was going to pass out or vomit, so I threw her to the linoleum flooring and kicked her away from me. She was still coherent. She still had the fighting urge to get away; she wanted to live. I decided to have some fun with her, so I rummaged through her kitchen drawers until I found a roll of duct tape, with which I used to tie off her hands and feet. I found the garage, and searched high and low for some rope, which I did find eventually above the washer and dryer. I ran back into the kitchen, and to my surprise I found three children with backpacks on, ages approximately 12, 10, and six, trying desperately to cut the duct tape wrapped around their mother. One of the little girls had on a tiara made of flowers, which I immediately recognized to be the lovely primrose.

At least she had good taste. That was an interesting situation for me, and frankly I had no idea what to do. The children did nothing wrong. They didn't like daisies as far as I knew. They didn't even know what was happening. I had to think fast, so I did what anyone would've done and I started yelling orders. "Get back! Get away from her! All of you, sit in a circle on the ground!" I duct-taped all three of them together in a circle, which made them immobile. I tied a thick noose out of the rope and hung it from the chandelier above the dining room table. I hoisted Alexandria up on top of the table, stood her up, and tied the noose tight to her neck. I'll never forget the look in her eyes. Complete and utter fear. She wasn't smiling anymore, I'll tell you that.

Poor little lady could barely reach the table. She was standing on her tippy-toes. Surprisingly, there was no screaming coming from anyone's mouths. The kids were sitting, as instructed, on the floor while their mother was talking with them from the ceiling. She was telling them how much she loved them and how she was going to be okay and how they were going to live wonderful lives. All bullshit. I wanted to explode and tell them the true meaning of life, and explain to them how shitty their lives were going to end up because they had parents that believed in the beauty of a DAISY! A fucking daisy! All the daisy represents is death. Daisies are the flower of death. But, I chose to withhold that information from them and let them learn the hard way.

To be honest, I felt extremely bad for the children. I saw myself in them, so I decided to make them some cheesy noodles that I found in the cupboard while I waited for their father to come home. That will forever be the most awkward 25 minutes I have ever endured. The boiling of the water, the cooking of the noodles, the serving of the food... If I had to do it again, I definitely would've skipped the macaroni dinner. However, I served these kids macaroni and cheese, and they all shook their heads like they didn't want it! How could they not eat my cheesy noodles that I worked so hard for?! Their mother told them to be polite and follow my instructions, so they agreed to eat my noodles. I spoon-fed all of them, because I wasn't about to remove the tape from their arms; I wasn't an idiot. That was the closest I ever came to having a child. I embraced every moment of it. I even made the little choo-choo sound of a train as I waved the spoon in front of their faces, and shoved the noodles into their teeny tiny mouths.

I got so lost in the magical moment of having a child, that I didn't even hear William's car door shut outside, and I didn't hear him open the front door, which is why I was so surprised when he came at me from behind with a baseball bat to the head. Luckily I came prepared for him and I brought my weapon of choice—a dagger.

I twisted that knife into his right side, which sent him falling to the ground next to his beautiful children. I stabbed him again in the arm, and one more time in the leg just to be sure he wouldn't try me again. I strung him up a nice little noose as well, and stood him up right beside his once-cheerful wife. I asked the kids, "Would you like to help me move the kitchen table?"

I wanted them to have the chance to participate in the killing of their evil parents. Believe it or not, the husband was the only one screaming and yelling and flailing his body all around. Alexandria looked at the kids and said, "Do as the man says, my loves." I removed the duct tape from their bodies and re-taped their feet so they couldn't run away. We each grabbed a corner of the table and slowly moved it from underneath the Simones' feet to the point where nothing was below them but air. There was a slight snapping sound, and then a couple of seconds later, I heard the same snapping sound again. The three children were crying their eyes out and grabbing onto their parent's feet trying to wake them up. Obviously they couldn't and they cried until no more tears were left. I had to figure out what to do with these three clueless, small people.

After a good 10-minute brainstorming session, I decided I would take them with me in my truck to the Lake of Wishes and I would tie a brick to each of their ankles and throw them in so that they could keep Bettie company. So, that's exactly what I did. I wrapped Alexandria and William up in a blanket and threw them in the bed of my truck, and squished all three of the kids next to me in the front.

I can't remember their names to save my life. I'm not even sure I ever knew their names. The sun had set by now, so I wasn't worried about anybody being a witness to what I was about to do that night. They were all so scared and clueless as to what to do that they did whatever I told them to do, so it was a quick, smooth process when I tied a brick to each of their little ankles and tossed them in one by one, as if I were feeding the ducks.

The whole process took around 15 minutes tops, and then I was on my way to bury their parents at Murphy Creek. At this point, I was so exhausted that I just wanted to curl up and fall asleep, but I persevered through to the end. I never re-turned to the flower shop to close up or to the graveyard to close the gate on time, but I wasn't worried about it. I assumed Blake could manage after all the times he had watched me do it. Little did I know I had the only key to the shop around a chain attached to my pants, so when I got to the yard to tidy up my business for the day, Blake was patiently waiting for me there. He ran up to me as soon as he saw my truck, and I started to panic. "Mr. Soyle, Sir, you have the key to the shop. I need it so I can close up." I told him not to worry about it and to just go home. I wanted to just be left alone at that point.

Unfortunately, for his sake, Blake happened to see Mrs. Simone's foot sticking out of the bed of my pickup, and immediately he started running. I was so exhausted. I didn't have the energy to kill a sixth person with my hands that day. So, I hopped in the driver's seat, started it up, and reversed at full speed, running Blake over with full force. He didn't see it coming. Hell! I didn't even see it coming.

Needless to say, this day in '74 was the closest my secrets ever came to being revealed. Six lives taken from the world in just one short day, and all of which were taken by *me*. I remember feeling so much power at that moment in time, so much power I almost didn't know what to do. I felt like I was getting in way over my head and I needed to skip back a couple steps. Up to that point, the meer killings of one or two a week seemed like a piece of cake. I had the entire system mastered to where I didn't even notice it. The illegal acts just blended into my everyday life and it felt like no one would ever catch on.

No one knew where the deceased were buried, no one suspected "Graham Soyle, the neighborhood flower shop owner" to be a murderer. I guess this particular day startled me a little bit. It made me realize that someone may actually catch on to the fact that six people went missing in one day, all of whom had a connection with me. Actually it scared me so much that after throwing Mr. and Mrs. Simone and Blake in the same hole, I shut the flower shop down for a little while. I figured if no one could order daisies from me, that would severely decrease my chances of running into a sticky situation. I thought it best to close up shop, just temporarily of course, and lay low for a bit until I felt comfortable again.

New Years Eve, 1978

What a great first New Year's with my new girlfriend, Riv. It was supposed to be our *first time* with one another. I was excited and wanted to make it special for her, ya know. Let her know she wasn't just some chick I wanted to have sex with. So I had prepared a home-cooked meal for her. I made shrimp linguini from a recipe book I kept from Bettie's house.

It was pretty simple so I knew that I could handle it, and then I also just threw some pre-made garlic bread in the oven, cause what girl doesn't love bread? I had also placed a bunch of rose petals in the shape of a heart all over the bed. I wanted to start dinner fairly early, 4:30 or 5:00, so we could have time to eat, make our way into the bedroom, do our thing, and also have time to go out and enjoy our first New Year's together. Scotty and his newlywed had a night planned out on the town. Which basically meant he was throwing a party at his bar, which was perfectly fine with me. I loved that place.

So the night was going pretty perfectly. We were sitting down at my dining room table, enjoying one another's company, getting to know each other. It was nice. Shortly after we finished eating, I suggested moving to the couch to be more comfortable. She agreed. That's when I put on my moves; my sweet talking. She bought into it as we vigorously made out the entire (short) walk down the hallway to my bedroom. I slowly turned her around, hugging her from behind, kissing her neck, showing off my heart-shaped roses on the bed. She quickly turned back around with a huge smile on her face, put her hands on my cheek, and continued kissing me.

From there, well I'm sure your imagination can fill in the rest. When we were finished, we did a bit of cuddling then got dressed and made our way to Scott's. Everyone was already pretty drunk; not surprising since it was about 10 o'clock by then. So we tried our best to catch up by just taking shots back to back to back. I had to cut River off after her second time vomiting. No one wants to deal with that. But we did successfully make it 'til midnight, and we had a wonderful kiss into the New Year. And what a New Year that was.

September, 1974

Since I was taking a break from the shop, I figured it was a good time to really start expanding my garden. That way I wouldn't be inclined to make any "home deliveries." So I went to Lloyd's Local store and bought all of the gardening essentials. I already had my peppers growing, so I decided to add some tomatoes, corn, and potatoes to place over top of Mr. Barker. Then once they were all going I wouldn't even need to go to the store for food; I'd just need to go to work. Not like food was much of a priority for me anyway. So that's pretty much what I did with my days for the next couple months. I worked my usual days at Murphy Creek, whilst also tending to my garden. Had my usual evening walks, rare visits to Scotty's bar for some Scotch and then spent my nights at home with my Little Kings and Dovals. I was staying quietly under the radar. Until that annoying nameless news article guy came knocking again.

Sunday, November 17th, 1974

I was in the midst of re-opening Lynn's Petals. I really didn't want people to forget about the place, and I thought two months was long enough. So I got restocked and just as I was about to unlock the doors some reporter came walking up behind me with his little yellow notepad and pen. He wanted to put an article in the paper about my shop, which I was excited about. He asked me about where I grew my flowers, where I got the name, and why people should shop at my store rather than the larger one in Dover.

I never did see that advertisement in the paper, but I figured it couldn't hurt, even if no one ever saw it. He left and I went on about my day. Not that it was busy—the word hadn't really gotten around yet that we were open again. So I basically just sat there all day organizing until about the very last hour this pretty lady came in wanting some tulips to take to her sister that was in the hospital. That was one of the things that I didn't care for about this business; everyone wants to tell you about their entire life story when they come in to buy flowers. But I found this girl attractive so I pretended that I cared. Her name was Sabrina, and we pretty much just talked the entire last hour I was open, mainly about her job as a third grade teacher at Meerdin Elementary. As I was closing up shop I asked if she wanted to go to Scotty's bar to have a drink and she agreed.

It wasn't too busy when we arrived so Scotty had plenty of time to socialize with us. Eventually though it was just basically only the two of them talking and flirting so I just ended up leaving them to it, which was fine because I had no interest in getting involved with anyone anyway. I had way too much going on. The next day when I stopped in for my Scotch shot, Scotty had plenty of gossip to tell me about the rest of their night together. I guess they ended up going home together and really hitting it off and from there they just started to see each other pretty steadily. Seemed she was always around. So I guess I'm glad that I was able to set them up together. *You're welcome, buddy.*

Monday, January 15th, 2007

I've been thinking a lot about Delilah today. Ya know how badly it hurts when you love someone, and then you no longer have them? Okay. Now, do you know how it feels to look at something and remember that person you loved? Pretty normal. Okay. Now, do you know how it feels to say something and immediately imagine that person's response? Okay, you're starting to understand now. So, for some of the more unfortunate groups—do you know how it feels to smell something, you start to feel your eyes slowly close, and you can instantly see them standing next to you? You can almost feel their breath on your skin? Talking to you? Smiling at you? Laughing? Now imagine feeling like that for about four or five consecutive years. Everything you do, everything you see or feel or touch or hear. Everything reminds you of that *one* person. Okay. So now you're beginning to be on the same page as me.

It's fucking miserable. And *then* just when you *think* you've gotten over them, someone mentions them to you, or asks something about them cause they're *curious*. Cause they don't *know*. They don't know what you've gone through, what you're *going* through. So you have to pretend, and then there they are again, stuck in your head, never leaving. That's your life.

Scotty and Sabrina's Wedding Day

Gee was that a depressing day. Ya know this was before I met River obviously, before I lost her, too... Anyways when I went to their simple wedding in Dover, I became super annoyed watching and smelling all the love in the air. As long as I knew him, Scotty never was a religious person, but Sabrina was. Not too over-the-top, ya know, like she didn't go to church every Sunday or Wednesday or anything. She just prayed on holidays before dinner and referred to God as an existing form. But she just *had* to get married under the roof of God... and the woman always gets what she wants on her wedding day apparently... so they tied the knot in the Christ Episcopal Church.

Small ceremony, only 10 or 15 people or so, and a couple random acquaintances that just came and sat to watch. I didn't know people actually did that, but it happened. They chose maroon and gray for their wedding colors. And they had everyone throw grains of rice at them when it ended as they walked away into their future together.

Watching her walk down the aisle in her cream-colored gown, with her overweight father, who could not have looked more disappointed,

I wouldn't say that I was jealous of Scotty. I was just jealous that he was starting the next chapter of his life, but I wasn't jealous that he was doing it with *her*. I found Sabrina very mediocre looking: stringy blond hair, thicker than desirable, and asymmetrical facial features.

My handsome friend, Scotty, definitely could've done better, but... good for him.

I was jealous of the way she looked at him and how he looked at her, and how they held hands, how they said "I do," how they kissed each other. Corny, I know, but I never got there in life.

I never had those special moments with somebody. Yeh I had my romantic relationships with Delilah, River, Fay; hell I'll throw Ingrid and Dawn in there just for fun. But, I never got to say "I do." I never had the chance to say, "I'm taken. I'm a married man."

Nope, been single my whole life and I still am and guess what? I'm gonna die single as well. Not much more I can tell you about their wedding other than it was simple, sad, and short. Figured it wouldn't last long, and... I mean... it didn't. I mean they probably would've still been together today IF Scott was still alive.

Too bad though.

MONDAY, JANUARY 15TH, 2007

Well it's been pretty boring here lately. No fight breakouts, no killings or suicides or releases recently. I've just kept to myself, trying to keep busy by writing, exercising, and eating I guess. That's about it.

Like I said, boring. So here is what a typical day looks like for us in here.

6:30 AM: *Wake up to the sound of a loud horn.* Most of the people in here don't even brush their teeth, but I can't live like that. I use the cardboard-bristled stick they give us to scrub away with my drinking water. Sometimes I even use my index finger... honestly it feels better on the gums.

6:30–6:45 AM: *Perform personal hygiene duties, make the beds, and suffer through the morning exercises.* Yeh, you're reading this right. Fifteen minutes to do all that. After brushing my teeth delicately, that usually leaves me with approximately eight minutes left to make the bed and do 50 pushups.

6:45–7:15 AM: *Leisure time for prisoners who were not involved with morning duties/first round of telephone calls.* I tried to always get the morning duties because I just wanted to get it over with. Obviously I never got any phone calls...

7:15–7:45 AM: *Breakfast (served only in my cell).* Typi-

cally, I am given barely-thawed blueberry oatmeal that
still contains ice crystals so that's how I know that
they microwave the damn stuff fresh out of the freezer
(and obviously they don't microwave it long enough).
Then, of course, I'm given a "biscotti" with jam, which
really translates to a crumbling rock with spreadable
mud on it. And last but not least, a small fruit cup,
usually peaches or oranges. That was my favorite part
of breakfast every day because it made me feel free.

7:45–8:15 AM: *Morning Roll-Call (in cells),* which was
never too exciting. Unless the powerful ones saw
something out of the ordinary, then in that case they
would flip the cell upside down just to piss off the prisoner. That only happened to me once, believe it or not.

8:15–8:30 AM: *The Grand Escort to my beautiful job
scrubbing toilets* where I did most of my thinking. You'd
think that would happen in my cell when I have nothing to do but stare at the wall, wouldn't you? No. Surprisingly, the whole toilet-scrubbing thing went a lot
faster when I filled my mind with thoughts.

11:30–11:31 AM: *Pass by my favorite prison ward, Alex*
He was a young boy. Very interesting looking, timid,
and friendly. Most of my prison mates took advantage
of him, but I saw potential in him. Every day I passed
him at the exact same time after leaving the toilets and
every day he was sporting a different hair style. Gel in
it one day, the next he would blow it out. He was an

open book and was the best part of my morning routine.

12:00–12:30 PM: *Lunch (served in my cell).* It isn't like all the stories you hear; ya know, the lines of prisoners getting served slop from the cafeteria crew and then sitting amongst your peers and enjoying thirty minutes of your life just a little bit. No. It was still slop, but they don't give you the pleasure of holding out the tray yourself and picking out a table. They serve it to you in your cell, just like breakfast. Usually lunch consists of a molded tuna sandwich, or a PB&J, or if I'm lucky, a grilled cheese. There is always a side—typically pinto beans, or mushed-up peas, and last but not least tap water. Or as I like to call it, toilet water.

12:30–1:00 PM: *Leisure time for prisoners who were not involved with afternoon duties/second round of telephone calls,* which happened to me at this time of the day. Most would assume leisure time was any prisoner's favorite part of the day. Well, I can tell you that it is most definitely not my favorite part. In fact, it is the time of the day I dread. Yeh I get to sit in my sorrows for a half hour, but, better yet, I get to do it outside! So I can hear the birds that I can't feed, and smell the flowers that I can't sell, and see the rainbows that I have no chance of chasing after. Leisure time is a joke. It lets me hold my life in my hand for 30 minutes with a clenched fist, but I never get to loosen my grasp. I never get to fully enjoy the life that I've been holding inside. I get to just stare at it and almost taste it but I never get to see it come to life.

1:00–3:30 PM: *The Grand Escort to the education part of the prison,*where I painfully endured lectures taught by unpaid volunteers on English grammar, U.S. history, speech, and other bullshit courses. Yeh, maybe that was great for the younger population of prisoners, but for me it was useless! I had been through this shit already. I don't need to listen to it all again...

3:45–4:15 PM: *Afternoon Roll-Call (in cells).*

5:00–5:30 PM: *Dinner (in cells)* or as I like to call it, brunchinner. "Dinner" is basically a compilation of foods that were leftover from the batches of food made for breakfast and for dinner and are thrown onto a tray with a glass of water and a cookie for dessert. Rarely, dinner is actually a different course, but when it is, it is usually a sloppy joe sandwich, which is one of the only foods here that is somewhat edible.

5:30–8:00 PM: *Leisure time for prisoners who were not involved with evening duties/third round of telephone calls,* so basically this is when people relax and go to the church or the tiny library. I spend my time usually writing this god-awful collection of feelings on my lined yellow paper. Truthfully, writing is the only thing I find any interest in, and, other than daydreaming of a life with Delilah, writing is what gets me to the end of each day. I can't wait until this time of day because it is the only free time I have to express myself. No one knows what I'm writing. No one really cares either. That's what I like about it—this journal is my own little secret full of secrets and one day everyone will know those secrets. But for now, they're mine. Only mine.

8:00–8:30 *pm Evening Roll-Call (in cells).*

8:30–6:30 *am: Bedtime.* The one good thing about being in prison... the sleep is incredible. Ten hours of sleep every single night, with no distractions or worries of what needs to get done the next day.

So let me tell you about the day they took me in...

Thursday, November 15th, 1984

I just left the shop and I stopped by Murphy Creek to lock the gates and collect the flowers I needed for the next day when I saw that damn figure again. That damn black figure that has been appearing in my life ever since I opened up Lynn's Petal's... ever since anything good ever happened in my life. Anyways, I told myself the next time I saw that dark-figured man again, I would approach him or her and find out what it was that they wanted with me. Most importantly, I wanted to find out who it was.

So, that's exactly what I did on November 15th, 1984. I'll

never forget that fucking date. Just like the state of Delaware never forgot what I did shortly thereafter. I charged at the black shadow of a man, afraid that he may try and run again. I cried out, "Please! Wait! How can I help you?" The man in black stopped dead in his tracks and slowly turned around. "My God!" I exclaimed, for I will never forget that moment for the rest of my life. I couldn't believe my eyes, because when the shadow turned around he revealed himself to be no other than Paul Robert Soyle, my good-for-nothing "father" whom I presumed to be dead up until that point. I was shocked. He was just standing there in the flesh 15 years older than I remembered him last, but other than that he looked like the same spineless man that beat Mama so many years ago. I remember our conversation as if I just had it with him five minutes ago...

"Son, I've been looking for you for a long time now. I can't believe you ended up in... Delaware," he said.

"And why exactly have you been searching for me?"

"I just wanted to talk to you. I've been so alone since... well that incident with your mother changed me forever. I also left town that day you bolted after the tragedy with your mom. I just didn't know what else to do." It was as if he thought I cared at all.

"I don't really give a shit. To be honest I thought I had gotten rid of you. What a disappointment this is."

"There is a reason I've been following you, trying to find you, my boy." Paul said without stuttering.

I responded with anger, "Don't call me 'your boy.' I will never be your son, and you most definitely will never be my father."

"Oh, get over yourself."

"Go ahead with your reason. Why have you been searching for me?"

He looked around with a mysterious mug on his face. "How about we take this inside? We can sit and catch up, maybe crack open a beer and get to know one another."

"I'm just fine standing here, thank you." I was getting increasingly annoyed. Not only did I never want to see my father again but now he was on *my* property, wasting my perfectly good day away. "So, I'll ask one more time, what do you want from me?"

"Well, to kill you," Paul said.

I turned and started running for my office, where I had a gun under the desk. I grabbed it and ran outside to defend myself. He stood there, with no weapon, just staring at me, as if he thought he could take me. How was he planning to kill me?

He shouted, "Before you shoot me, just tell me why. Why did you take her from me?"

"I didn't take her from you. You took her from me!" At first I was so angry that tears started falling down my cheeks.

"No Graham, *you* killed her."

Hysterically crying, I responded with, "You hit her so hard so many times! I couldn't bear to let you hit her another time. She was practically begging me to kill her."

He looked at me with anger and sadness and said "Sha-ame on you-u," and before he could finish that wonderful sentence, I shot him. Killed him for sure this time. Two bullets straight into the skull, and down he went.

I slowly started to raise the gun up to my head and think

about how easy it would be. One movement of the finger and everything would go away. Pull the trigger and there would be no more confusion, no more pain, no more secrets. But before his head could even hit the ground, six police cars came rushing around the corner and two men put handcuffs around my wrists. They came so fast, almost as if they were waiting around the corner waiting for me to kill him. He set me up. But why? Did he want to die? How did he know I would do it? Or maybe he didn't know. Maybe he was just looking for a confession. Either way, he got both. Bet the police had a field day with that one. It was only minutes later before I was watching Murphy Creek get smaller and smaller behind me as the police car drove me away. I often wonder if I had just let him come inside and talk, like he wanted to, if things would have turned out like that. Perhaps that is all he wanted was to know me. But I was too stubborn to let him, and now he's dead and I'm stuck in here.

Moral of the story is don't kill people. Actually, that *should* be the moral of the story, but really the true meaning of that statement is don't get *caught* killing anybody. Unfortunately because of that bastard, I ended up getting 20 years to life for the murder of Lynn Marie Soyle and Paul Robert Soyle. Luckily I was just waiting for the day that they would catch me for *something* so I had already written up a letter leaving my shop and cemetery to Vern. At least he would still have something to keep him occupied while I was gone.

Let me tell you that riding in the back of a police car, handcuffed, is just as wonderful as it sounds when you hear about it in stories. I felt claustrophobic, I felt angry, I felt betrayed, I felt like my entire life was stripped from me.

That's still how I feel to this day, actually, because guess what? Still here.

Still serving time for the murder of Mr. and Mrs. Soyle. Bullshit. I mean the law system doesn't take into account the circumstances of their deaths. Paul was a piece of shit and deserved to die and the jury should take that into account, and Mama was in so much pain, she begged me to take her life. I tried to explain this to the court, but no! They didn't care to hear anything but the bad things. They tell you that, "You have the right to remain silent. Anything you say can and will be used against you in a court of law...blahblahblah." Yeh they tell you that, but it's not what they actually mean. Once you're arrested, you have no fucking rights. None.

They dragged me by the arm into the jail, and brought me up to the desk to submit booking information. The lady working the registration desk was named Primrose, and she had this grin on her face that made me want to slap it off. She was like those women that are way too nice to you that everyone loves and you can't figure out why. Yeh, that was Primrose. Good thing her name wasn't Daisy... would've slapped a lot more than just her smile off of her.

Graham Embry Soyle
01/15/07

DAISY

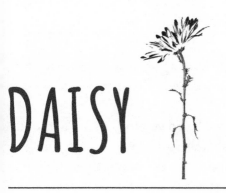

Innocence and Purity

This is the last of it. It's the last thing you're going to read because there is nothing more after this. Don't expect too much cause I only have so much to give, and I'm not a professional so this is pretty much it.

Sorry. No wait, I'm not sorry. I stopped writing because it kills me every time you fall into the words that spill all over this piece of paper. No matter how hard I've tried, I've never been able to forget you all.

It's funny how, as kids, saying "sorry" was such a huge deal. But now, 'sorry' doesn't mean anything...I'm sorry. See? Everything's the same. I am sorry and I mean it and it doesn't change a thing. You're still you and I'm still me.

Except we're completely different from the "you and me" that I remember so vividly. I stopped writing because you never said that "sorry" that I needed so badly to hear. The "sorry" that I've said over and over again that didn't impact anything. I wish I could tell myself sorry that it took so long to realize what you did to me.

I stopped writing because I loved you for so long without knowing it. You knew. You all knew and you didn't tell me. You knew and you let it happen. You knew and then you broke me into pieces that will never be put back together again. You knew and now here I am, finally ending that pain, cause now I'm too tired to ever be sorry again.

Chandeliers are what I imagine the gates to Heaven look like. Shiny and bright and right in your face, but yet they are out of reach.

Then there's a small chance that as soon as you're about to reach the brightness, it comes crashing down upon you, sending you to a new place, figuratively and physically. You all know me pretty well by now: you know I've never been one to be sure of my faith.

I've never known if I believe in God or not. At this point in my life, I can't say I will ever come to that epiphany, so I'm left to do one thing before I die. I can either choose to believe or choose not to believe. I've had a lot of time to think about this. Actually 23 years.

I've decided that if there is a Heaven, all the people that I have ever loved will be there. The only way for me to see Delilah again is to make it to Heaven. I am choosing religion in my final days as a last attempt at love. So, I have decided I'm going to head to the chapel tonight and beg for forgiveness and speak of my sorrows and my sins.

I hope that these letters I have written will also help in my plea towards God to forgive me and let me in through the shiny chandelier-like gates. But somewhere there is a beach that time cannot reach. Where everyone and everything has always been and never was. And perhaps you are there waiting for me. In that place, time cannot touch. See you soon, Delilah.

MONDAY, JULY 4TH, 1993

The day I executed my last kill. Well, my life isn't over just yet so who knows? I may kill another, but... I'm not planning on it, so that would make Ray the last man I murdered up to this point in time. Ray was my cellmate 14 years ago. I managed to make it the first nine years in the mansion without ever getting assigned a roommate... until Ray turned up. He was placed in cell block D with me and I didn't like him from the moment the bad men escorted him in. He looked slimy, like he looked like the type of man I would keep far away from my daughter if I had one.

His name was Raymond Maldaris and he was only 26 years old. He had greasy brown hair and a twitch that made both of his eyes and his right hand move in a creepy way. He darted for the top bunk, like he wasn't even gonna ask or anything—he was just gonna take the top half. As if he had been there for years before I had and owned the right to everything... what an idiot he was... I sleep on the bottom bunk anyways because I'm scared of falling off, but that's not the point. The point is that he actually had the audacity to just steal something from somebody else and not even think twice about it. Yeh. I know I stole flowers from the dead for most of my young adult life, but at least I knew what I was doing was wrong. I thought twice about it for sure... every time. Getting back to Ray... everyone in the mansion had this phrase they would hum or sing whenever Ray got too close:

> *"Hey! Ray! Go away!*
> *Go play! Go lay! Whaddya say?*
> *May you get out of my way*
> *And have a gay day!"*

Kinda sad really, but nevertheless, I joined in on these chants and played along because I just didn't like the guy. No one really ever got to know him except for me. Ya know I got to share every night with him and we talked sometimes. Everyone thought he was a pedophile but I found out the real reason he was locked up in here with me.

He robbed a grocery store back in his hometown. Said he killed a couple unintentionally during the incident, but that he ultimately just needed money for his wife and three kids at home. Not the best reputation to have in a palace like this but better than feasting on little children like everybody thought. He was just a family guy who didn't have enough money. I learned to respect Ray for who he was and he became my friend. We used to stay up and talk about our lives back home before we got thrown in here.

He told me about his hilarious kids and his beautiful wife and he really seemed full of hope and happiness for a while. Until his court hearing... poor Ray ended up getting sentenced to life. Everything changed after that. It's like he gave up trying to get through the day because he didn't have anything to look forward to anymore. His family stopped visiting him, he stopped talking, he went back to being the crazy Ray that everybody made fun of in the corridors. That's when he asked me...

Raymond asked me to kill him. Now, this was new territory for me... I was used to being the one to make decisions. I didn't like being told what to do, but I felt sorry for my friend. He claimed he couldn't do it himself because he needed to be 100 percent sure he made it to Heaven.

S'pose I don't blame him. Ya know I'm in that very situation right now, and I figured since he never did anything wrong in his life, why start then? I had already soiled my chances so I wasn't losing anything by helping him out. Still, I didn't necessarily *want* to get caught with his murder, so I tried to hide it as best I could which meant, unfortunately for Ray, he was going to struggle a bit. Early that morning around two o'clock I grabbed the flat, discolored pillow from behind his warm neck and swiftly placed it over his mouth and nose. His eyes were barely poking out over the top of the pillow, but I could see that they looked happy. They looked relieved. Of course he struggled a bit; I mean it's natural instinct to survive, but eventually he gave up fighting because he was so close to death. He was ready.

Strangely enough, during that moment I felt very spiritual and I wanted to boost his chances of making it through the gold gate at the end of the tunnel, so I said a prayer as I took his life. I said a prayer for him. I said a prayer for me. I just wanted God to know that Ray was a good man, and that I was a good man for doing him a favor that he could not. I remember shedding a tear as I felt my prison mate go limp and disappear from the world. I placed the murder weapon back under his now-lifeless neck and brought my tears to bed.

Oh, what I would give to be young, charming, 21-year old Graham again! Now, I find myself shaking and unable to lay down and sit up without my whole body aching. I miss the good body aches. Ya know I would get them after digging too many graves one day or after killing one of my many victims. I would wake up one morning after drinking too much the night before and not be able to move.

Those were the good body aches and I miss them so much. I would do anything to live one more day as Graham Soyle, graveyard/flower shop owner. Sometimes I wish I could just start my life over and do it all again. Really do it right this time. Ya know, people say money can't buy happiness, but... I mean... I feel like it definitely could. If I could control every aspect of my life from the very beginning, who knows how my life would've turned out.

From the beginning...hmm...let's see: I would have two happily married parents. Mama and my real father, Keith Windom. Obviously he wouldn't die in a car accident on the night of my birth in this little fantasy life I am creating, and Mama and Keith would happily bring me home to their two-story suburban California dream home where I would grow up in a wonderful cul-de-sac and be surrounded by well-behaved, normal children like myself.

My name wouldn't be Graham though... fuck, I was always being teased for being a "cracker" when I was in school. I have no idea what was running through Mama's head when she settled with that horrific title. Probably Paul's idea. Anyways, back to the fantasy...Graham would never even be an option for my name. My name would be something majestic, but also under the radar, something like... Damien? Yeh, sure. Damien Embry Soyle. Yes I'm aware that "Soyle" wasn't Keith's last name, so technically I wouldn't have it in this fantasy life. *However,* this is all made up anyways so I can make anything happen. Besides, I like "Soyle" as a last name, so I'm gonna keep it, thank you very much. Mama and Daddy would have a baby girl a few years later and name her Peaches.

Mama is a stay-at-home mother and Keith is a big corporate leader at some advertising agency, but he is always home for dinner by 5 PM. Our little dream family has a dog that is basically Gene and he lives forever, along with our squishy-faced orange cat named George. See, Damien Soyle in *this* magical life will accomplish great things like becoming the sergeant of the police force in Los Angeles, he will be happily married with five children, and he will have a garden of daisies surrounding his three-story home.

He will travel abroad and live life to the fullest, maintaining a healthy relationship with his family and friends until he dies peacefully at the age of 82. See how different my life would have been if death hadn't followed me my whole life and money had taken the place of death? But that is not how my life turned out! So, no one can be mad at me for making the most of what I had, which is exactly why I would do anything to be 21-year-old Graham again. That was the peak of my shitty life, and I'd like to return to the top. If a big pile of shit is all that is offered to you, wouldn't you climb to the top of the pile and sit on it and look down at all the other bitches swimming in the shit at the bottom? That is exactly what I did.

"Why did he have to pick those damn flowers? Why did he have to bring them into her and set them in a vase beside her on the table? Why did he have to whisper something in her ear like a doting husband who loved her? Why? Why three white fucking daisies every single time? Why?" You know how many times I tried to burn that daisy bush outside? How many times I tried to yank each stem out of the ground and hope they would never grow back? A lot. A shit ton of times, actually!

I tried desperately to get those daisies out of my life and I failed each and every time. That daisy bush was relentless! They grew back fuller and whiter than before every single time! Perhaps I wouldn't be so screwed up in the head if it wasn't for those daisies?

Who knows what I would've done with my life if it wasn't for the mere daisy? Daisies represent murder! They represent how ugly the world truly is!

Anyone that picks daisies like my good-for-nothing father deserves nothing less than death! Anyone that asks for daisies deserves death! Anyone that calls themselves Daisy (as if that is even a good name) deserves death!

Anyone who mentions a daisy in a respectable manner deserves to die. Daisies destroy devotion and disassemble relationships of love.

To whoever finds this

Tonight my metaphorical bottle of emotions has finally over-filled. I am in the midst of panic. This should be pretty simple, huh? After everything that I've done, well, why would it be hard for me to kill myself? Although I'm sure that's what everyone thinks, huh? That it's going to be easy. But have you ever talked to someone who tried and failed? How much they immediately regretted even attempting it?

How grateful they are that they never succeeded? I feel like an astronaut stranded in space. I suppose I don't really have anyone specific to write this to, or leave it for, or to tell *I love* you or *I'm sorry* for the last time, too.

And it's not like anyone in this good-for-nothing place gives a damn about me. I sure don't have any family. No wife or kids or friends waiting for me to get out.

So I think it's about time to just give up. I've been thinking about this for a couple weeks now. I just can't deal with the unbearable misery this place puts me through. At first I believed suicidal thoughts were a passing phase, something I would be able to wake up from or shake off. But I soon found out that the idea of dying just wouldn't go away. The visions of death won't stop. One million things run through my head but I just can't think of what to say.

I lay here in bed thinking about how I could go about it, what resources I have in here to accomplish what I want, and I think that I've decided to just do it the old-fashioned way; hanging.

I guess I'll just use my shirt and tie it to the top bar of the cell door, and I'll have my lovely cellmate there to make sure I don't pussy out. So yeh, that's that.

Now I am just patiently awaiting the relief that death will bring me. I hope whoever hands my life story ends up in, enjoys it.

At least I won't have been a complete waste. Who knew something as simple as a daisy could turn someone into such an innocent psychopathic murderer. Forgive me if I was a disappointment.

Graham Embry Soyle
01/17/07

Hey Vern, remember me? Graham? Or Soyle, like you preferred to call me. Long time, no talk, am I right? How are things? How's Murphy Creek? How's my flower shop? Not like I'm going to get to read the response to those questions... Well, unfortunately the time has come for me to tell the truth about some things, and you're the only person I trust will do what needs to be done. So listen carefully. I've done some pretty fucked-up things in my life, Vern. I don't need you to judge me for what I've done, so let's get that straight. With this letter, I am sending a "book" or a collection of my journals that I've written in prison. Oh yeh by the way, I'm locked up... I'm sure you knew that though... I'm sure everyone back home knows that... anyways it'll all make sense to you after you read what I wrote though. I need you to take what I've written and release it to the press or to a publisher or something. I need the world to see what I did. I need the world to know my name or it was all for nothing. Please. Also attached are nine letters to people I care about. None of them are alive anymore, so I need you to track down their families and mail the letters to them. It is so important that they receive the letters and see how sorry I am for everything. Send them all a copy of the journals, too.

You're going to wonder why I am choosing you for all of this and the answer is I don't know. I've always felt strongly connected to you in some way. You just mind your business and you live your life the way you want to live it and I respect that so much. I know you're blind and this is going to be really hard for you to do on your own, so please choose someone you trust to help you. I trust you enough to trust who you choose. Thanks for being a part of my life and I'll see you in the afterlife.

I love you. I love you, Delilah.

I love you more than you will ever know, more than I ever told you.

Sometimes I like to envision my life if everything had been different, if everything had been normal and okay. If I had had a normal childhood, or if I had had a normal father figure.

Then maybe, just maybe, I would've been a normal kid. I would've still met you the same way and fell in love the same way. I like to envision a life where I'm not crazy.

I see you in that life, Delilah. We would've lived a long, marvelous life together, full of happiness, newborn babies, and achievement.

Unfortunately, you don't get to choose your life, you don't get to choose the parents you are given or the brain that God creates for you.

I know this letter will never reach you, but I hope it brings happiness to someone close to you who receives it.

I want you to know that I will join you soon in Heaven and we will be able to live out the marvelous life I had always dreamed we would have.

I will live a new life in Heaven. A life absent of death, crime, sorrow, and unluckiness.

You are what has helped me through this entire experience and helped me survive to the end of each and every day. I will be with you soon, my love.

I am so terribly sorry that our perfect life together that we pictured was ruined and I hope you will allow me to create new memories with you.

Oh Riv! I will always love you, River.

You hold a special place in my heart because you allowed me to live the wonderful life I dreamed of living with Delilah.

For a moment at least...You supported me, you stood up for me, you provided alongside me, and we shared many laughs and cries together.

Hell we even made a baby together. That wasn't born, of course, but still.

Very special.

I could've grown to love you like I love Delilah. Really, I was reaching that place with you.

And yes, you had to go and destroy that possibility for the both of us, but I can forgive you.

I am trying this new thing now at the end of my life where I am trying to be positive and I'm trying to forgive.

Just know that I did have fun with you for the time that we were together but ultimately you were just someone to fill the void for my everlasting love, Delilah Ann Taylor.

I just want to apologize to you and tell you how sorry I am that your life ended the way that it did.

I love you.

I love the times we had and although this will never reach you, I want you to know that my life is about to end.

However that makes you feel.

I'm not sure, but I just wanted you to know.

Hello, my name is Graham.

Nice to meet you.

You didn't even know my name the whole time we knew each other, but yet you've impacted my life so much, I am forced to write this letter to you. Daisy, I am so sorry. You're the relationship that I regret the most.

You didn't deserve what happened to you.

You didn't deserve to be given the name "Daisy." I mean, for all I knew, you hated your name as well, but you never had the opportunity to tell me because I never gave you the chance.

My angry side came out before you had the chance, and I'm sorry.

I loved the idea of you.

I loved the idea of you so much and you reminded me of my true love, Delilah.

I wanted you so bad, I wanted her so badly, and I had you for one night. Your last night...

Please forgive me like I forgive you.

My Dearest Bettie,

Oh how I wish you could be here with me now to tell me I'm being irrational, to tell me not to go through with it.

I loved you so much. You were the mother figure that I needed when I didn't have one anymore.

I wanted to do good things for you, I wanted to make you proud, but when you left me, I let you down. And I'm sorry Ms. Bettie, I'm so sorry... I want you to be proud of me again and I want you to love me like the son you never had the chance to have with Walter. I hope you're with him in Heaven and I hope you two will take Delilah and myself into your little life up there and allow us all to be a little family.

I now understand why you wrote me that letter before you sunk yourself to the bottom of the world.

I get it, cause no matter dead or alive, it feels good expressing my feelings to someone.

You inspired me to write my own letters. So thank you Bettie, truly, thank you so much for everything.

I took good care of your graveyard when you were gone, I promise. Despite the crimes that took place there, it still is a good, pure, peaceful setting that people enjoy coming to.

I left it in the hands of blind old Vern, and I trust him with my life.

I love you Bettie, and I will see you soon.

Dear Keith Windom, Dad...

I'm not sure how to even start this letter to you because for one, I've never actually spoken to you so I'm not sure how your voice sounds or what you even look like... and I never will know. Secondly, I'm not sure what I even want to say to you. I know you will never see this letter, but this is helping me get to a better place.

This letter to you is helping me close my life out and open the doors to a better ending. I would like to say I love you.

Well I know I love you more than the good-for-nothing piece-of-shit father I was given instead of you. I love stories of you and I love the being of you inside of me. The good parts of me were created from you and Mama. I was formed to be bad based off of many things, one of them being your death, which is why I am terribly sorry that I killed you.

Daddy, I am so sorry that I was the one that ended your life. If only I could have just stayed inside of Mama for just one more day, who knows where we all would be now. If I had decided to enter the world a day earlier even, I may be sitting at the dinner table with you now, creating memories.

But no. My selfish ass wanted to enter the world when I did, and as a result, I lost you. If I could take anything back, it would be that moment. I would give anything to meet you and there is nothing I can do about it now.

All I can do is say how sorry I am and hope that it gets me to a better place where I can be with you. Please take care of my Mama if you're up there with her, and I'll talk to you later.

Mama, this is hard for me to say, even if it isn't to your face.

Be glad I took your life when I did because you would've been heartbroken to see how I've ended up.

I'm in jail, Mama. I'm in jail for murder, and I've been here for a long time. I get out soon though, and I wanted to tell you that I am going to take my own life. I am going to take my own life because I don't deserve to be out in the world after everything I've done.

I wrote everything down that I've ever done and apologized to those I hurt, including you. I'm sorry Mama for being a bad seed and growing up to do terrible things because that is not how you raised me. You raised me to be good.

I destroyed your name when I named my flowershop business after you. I am so sorry. At this point, it is too hard for me to take you with me into the afterlife, so I need to say goodbye to you forever.

I need to end on a good note and stop feeling guilty for the sorrow I caused you. Although you'll never see this, just know that I love you so much. I love you so much that I must let you go. I know that you are with Keith in Heaven, and I hope you two will have a blissful eternity together.

And yes, Mama, I mentioned Heaven. I know how badly you wanted me to believe in Him, and I want you to know that I have found the faith you always hoped I'd have.

I now believe I will be led down the best path after my life has ended. I love you Mama, and I will never forget you. I am your only son and you are my only mother and we have a bond that will never break. Goodbye.

Paul.

You were a part of a significant portion of my life. I don't have many apologies to make to you. However, if I had to choose one, it would be to say sorry for taking Mama away from you... from us. It wasn't your fault that you had a disease.

And I know deep down that you truly loved her.

I can't imagine the heartbreak you must have went through losing the love of your life. I understand that feeling and it's awful.

But you were an asshole that beat me and my beautiful mother. How do you do that to someone?

All I wanted was a normal childhood and you just had to go fuck that up for me.

Look at me now: you ruined my life, and for what? So you could have a few drinks when you got home from work?

I hope it was worth it. I wish you hadn't ever come looking for me, and most importantly I wish you hadn't ever found me.

I had everything running smoothly and exactly how I wanted it and you just waltzed into my life and ruined that, too.

I've been stuck in this hellhole because of you and I don't forgive you for that.

But regardless, I am sorry for that one thing.

That's all. Goodbye.

Hey Scotty, man do we have a past.

I miss ya brother. I think about you all the time. If I only had one apology to give it would probably be to you. You were the only person that was always there for me. You were my friend when I moved to a new city, you were the person I would come to after a long day of work; Scotty. Scotch. Scotty. Scotch. Scotch. Scotty, Scootch!!

The guy I'd want to tell everything to when something new ever happened. You were there through thick and thin and never left my side the entire time I was in Meerdin.

I took you for granted and I'm sorry. I wasn't there for you the way you were for me and I'm sorry. You were always honest to me and I wasn't to you... and I'm sorry. I loved you and I never did anything about it. How is anyone supposed to know the truth if you don't ask or tell?

Now I'll never know, and although I'm not completely okay with that, there's nothing I can do about it now. That's why I'm so sorry. I'm sorry for taking away what we could have had. I'm sorry for pretending, for years, like I was okay and I wasn't. For living a lie. I'll never forgive myself, and now you can't either. Killing you was the hardest for me.

I wanted you so bad to just join my side. We would've been a force to be reckoned with! You and I, in the business together. Roommates, having fun for the rest of our lives.

But no, you, just like everybody else, saw the bad in me and I had to eliminate you. I'm sorry our lives didn't work out in the way they could've.

My Dear Gene,

I've missed you so much. It took a long time to get over you.

I always felt like it was my fault that you left me, but I realize now that it was just life.

You would be so disappointed in me, so for that I'm sorry.

I should have been better, and maybe if I was you would have never gotten sick and died on me.

But I thank you for all the mental support you gave me for the time we had together.

You helped me through more than I could ever imagine.

Love ya buddy.

EPILOGUE

K eith Laverne Windom, born 1922, was a passionate lover and a strong fighter. He fell in love with Lynn Marie Soyles, born 1920, and conceived a child with her in the year of 1946. After a devastating car accident on the way to the hospital on the night of Graham's birth, Lynn was extracted from the vehicle long before Keith because she was at high risk due to her active labor. Mr. Windom was taken to another hospital outside of town due to overcrowding issues at Topeka East Clinic. Lynn had to deal with the exciting delivery of her new baby boy and the devastating news that the man she had been traveling in the truck with was declared dead at the scene all in one night. This news was told to her by several nurses and policemen who confirmed he had no pulse when they arrived at the accident.

However, this was not the case. Keith Windom lay in a coma at Topeka Memorial for the next 1,119 days. Keith and Lynn were not married. They had nothing connecting the two of them together... no one really knew the two of them were even seeing each other at the time, so of course no one contacted Lynn when he finally did awake. Life went on for Lynn. She settled down in Kansas with Paul and began to raise her child.

When Keith did wake, he remembered everything about his life and wanted it back. He tried to contact Lynn and even managed to locate her. He went to visit her and saw that she had a husband and a small child and a house to take care of. She had created a life for herself and she seemed happy to him, so he made the hard decision to let her be happy and not get involved. He didn't want to be with anyone else though. His true love was Lynn. Keith had nothing to his name and never wanted Lynn to surprisingly run into him one day and be reminded of their life together, so he decided to hitchhike across the country until he found a place to reside.

Keith, who now called himself Vern, found himself in Meerdin, Delaware, outside of the Meer Murphy Creek grave-yard. He liked the area and the people in the town, so he decided to stay put for a while. The owners of the graveyard, the Murphys, would give him food and blankets and made sure he was comfortable on the streets. After a couple of years of getting to know Vern the homeless man, the Murphys decided to offer up their shed on the property. They agreed to allow Vern to live there, as long as he helped around the yard from time to time. Vern agreed and became their right-hand man. He became a professional at digging holes and raking and tending to the gravesites. He soon became Vern the gravedigger and loyal employee and, most importantly, a friend to the Murphy family. He had a small limp and partial blindness from his accident but he never revealed that piece of information to his friends. He just let them believe he was born that way because he didn't want to bring up his past as it would make him regret his decision to leave Lynn be.

Years went on and all that was left of the Murphy family was Bettie, the youngest daughter. The graveyard became too much for her to take on by herself so she hired a young gravedigger that we all grew to love by the name of Graham. Vern and Graham became very close over the years and had a special connection. They shared similar interests of animals and flowers and music and treated each other like family. Little did they know, they were actually father and son.

See, Graham always believed that his real father died on the night of his birth in a horrific car accident and Vern never expected his son to turn up at the exact place of his home, so they never caught on. Until Vern read Graham's novel...

For some reason, Graham trusted Vern enough to allow him to handle his goodbyes and make his crimes public. He wanted the world to know what he did and he wanted Vern to be the one to share the news. There was an unexplainable connection between the two of them and he knew he could have faith in his friend to follow through. Laverne received the thick envelope full of Graham's life and the many apology letters that went with it. It took him a few days to read everything because he had trouble seeing, but by the second page, he knew. He knew that Graham was his son. He didn't know what to think; if he should be happy or sad or angry.

In one way, Vern was ecstatic to learn that he actually did know his son. He got to experience his entire young adult life with him and watch him grow into a hardworking man. But on the other hand, his son was a serial killer. He created a man that committed so many terrible crimes. He felt guilty for not being there to lead him in the right direction as his father. The shock of all of these emotions flowing out all at once sent him into a state of mental instability. Keith Laverne Windom did not wake up after that night.

Graham's apology letters never surfaced to the mourning family members. His confessions and life story never made public view, as they were all just taken as belongings of an old man who died in his sleep. Those bodies still lay hidden amongst the yard to this day and the missing members of Meerdin were never uncovered.

Graham's suicide attempt was successful and he died not knowing that he had known his real father his entire life. He also died believing that he confessed all his sins to the world and made peace with God in his last days, but that is not the case. Instead, the one final act he performed in his life was sending the message to his father that ended up killing him. Graham Embry Soyle managed to kill another man, even in death. He was born to kill, and kill is what he did.

Graham was always remembered in Meerdin as being the charming gravetender and business owner who respected his elders and treated everyone with sincerity. Even though he murdered his parents and admitted to it, everyone still felt bad for him. A lot of people showed up to his service to say their final goodbyes to the unfortunate suicidal young man. Apparently, the members of the town collectively decided his favorite flower was the daisy, so they buried him in the same soil as all of his victims, with a large headstone reading, *"May he rest amongst the daisies, 1946 – 2007."*

ABOUT THE AUTHORS

NATALIE
TOWNSEND

JESSICA
HUTCHINSON

Many years ago two young ladies met through family and became friends. Jessica, living in Colorado and Natalie, living in Florida, both had careers in the medical field but still had plenty of free time for fun.

One night together after a strange dream and a bottle of white wine, *Naked Graves* was born. They spent four years pouring their hearts onto these pages whenever they found spare time. As an avid traveler, a lover of cats, and a passionate storyteller, Natalie has always enjoyed writing. She graduated from the University of South Florida with a bachelor's in health sciences and a minor in German.

Jessica furthered her schooling from phlebotomy to supervising mobile blood banking. She spent most of her younger years traveling across the U.S., writing poetry and song lyrics, but never had the confidence to further it more than her bedside journal.

Overloaded with doubt and exhaustion they almost gave up, but they continued to combine their collaborating minds and held onto their extreme dedication. The two of them turned their ideas into a 70k-word masterpiece.

This might be their first book, but it certainly is not their last.

We thank you for reading!

Made in United States
Orlando, FL
11 February 2022

14712672R00161